Scribe

Also by Alyson Hagy

Novels
Boleto
Snow, Ashes
Keeneland

Stories
Ghosts of Wyoming
Graveyard of the Atlantic
Hardware River
Madonna on Her Back

Scribe

A Novel

Alyson Hagy

Graywolf Press

This publication is made possible, in part, by the voters of Minnesota through a Minnesota State Arts Board Operating Support grant, thanks to a legislative appropriation from the arts and cultural heritage fund, and through grants from the National Endowment for the Arts and the Wells Fargo Foundation Minnesota. Significant support has also been provided by Target, the McKnight Foundation, the Amazon Literary Partnership, and other generous contributions from foundations, corporations, and individuals. To these organizations and individuals we offer our heartfelt thanks.

Published by Graywolf Press
250 Third Avenue North, Suite 600
Minneapolis, Minnesota 55401

www.graywolfpress.org

Published in the United States of America

ISBN 978-1-55597-818-1

2 4 6 8 9 7 5 3

Library of Congress Control Number: 2018934486

Cover design: Kimberly Glyder

Cover art: June Glasson, *J. S.*

For Mandy Hoy,
who struck the spark

Scribe

Salutations

The dogs circled the house all night, crying out, hunting. She knew they were calling to her. Beckoning. Working their churn. The world she lived in had become a gospel of disturbances, and the dogs wouldn't let her forget that. In the morning, before she had even gone to the springhouse for milk, she saw a man waiting at the foot of her garden. It was how they did.

Summer had spun away from them all. The creek banks were whiskered with a nickel-shine frost, and she could smell the cooking fires laid down by the ones who called themselves the Uninvited. Pig fat and smoke. Scorched corn. There were more people at the camp every week, staking out tarps, drying fish seined from the river. They were drawn to her fields at the end of their seasonal migrations because of what had happened there some years before, because of their beliefs. She did not know if they planned to stay for the winter.

The man's clothes were rust-rimmed and deflated. He wore a battered straw hat. Those who wanted something from her arrived at the brick house above the creek—the Doctor's House they called it, a remnant from her father's time—and waited for her, always alone. She didn't care for ceremony, but ceremony was what they needed. Their silent arrival was part of a code they passed among themselves. It was the same for the Brubaker woman who prepared the bodies of the dead and the man from Jack's Mountain who was known to hoard crystals of salt.

The dogs began to gather. The swift brindle one, then the fawn bitch, then the rat catcher with its long, shredded ears. There were only three this time. Each bore fresh wounds. The fawn bitch, blood threaded through its eager saliva, leaned hard against her knees. It was a disrespectful habit, one that couldn't be tolerated. Animals and neighbors had to be taught their limits. She struck the bitch on the ribs with her wooden staff. The bitch yelped and went to its haunches, but it didn't leave her. None of them did.

She raised her palm and signaled to the man. You are welcome at my home, she signed. It's the time of barter and trade.

The man showed neither a pistol nor a blade. He had put his weapons aside in order to make his plea. She, herself, had given up arms some time ago. Everyone knew who she was and what she had to offer. They understood she kept nothing in the brick house anyone would want to steal.

He began to walk toward her, past the twine looped and snared around her plucked garden, past the skeletal stalks of her harvested corn. He was holding items outward for display, objects filched smoothly from his pockets. There was a stick of split wood. And what might be a precious shrivel of tobacco. These were his offerings.

"I seen you pulled a good crop of squash and beans," the man said. "I seen your vines. It's been a good year."

"It has," she said, carefully. "A good year. Are you thirsty?"

"I ain't," the man said. "I been down to your creek first thing. It's a good creek."

"It can be," she said. "I have sweet spring water, too. I can make you a tea."

"No need," the man said, looking at the blind face of her house from under his hat. His eyes appeared to be sleep-sore and yearning. His feet scuffed the tangled grass. "I brung what they say you might take in payment. I come to ask if you will write me a letter."

He raised his forearms in an awkward, stilted way—as if his request had set its own barbs into him—and she took the stick of wood, and the dangling twist of tobacco. It was a generous offer. He wished to trade a supply of split hardwood, enough for the winter, and a bundle of tobacco cured in the old way. The man didn't look prosperous, no one did these days, not this far from the cities. Still, he was willing to barter things of value. The fawn bitch circled him once, its damp nose carried high in the air.

"I ain't from here," the man said, bowing his head as if she might expect that. "But I heard about you. My wife was raised at Snow Creek, where you're known to help people in need. You make keen and proper letters, and you can write out a man's pain and ease it from his heart forever, that's what they say. I'll cut the wood myself. I seen strong black oak up on that ridge of yours. And maple, too. I brung the tobacco with me."

"Let's rest on the porch," she said. The dogs were no longer paying attention to the man, no more than if he were a dusty cedar tree or a flood-stained shelf of granite. He didn't stink of threat or guile. Not to them.

"I left a stone at the place by the road bridge," the man said, looking back over his shoulder. "I done it after nightfall, soon as I arrived. Just like I was told. Is it true what they say about the woman and the miracles she made here?"

"Some of it is true," she said. "I leave her a stone whenever I cross. We all do."

The man wasn't as old as she first believed. Fortysome. He said his name was Hendricks. He had spent time in uniform fighting enemies both foreign and domestic. That was how he said it. Domestic. He'd grown up just over the Carolina line.

"I done my share of migrations when I was young," he told

her. "I was born before the war and didn't have much choice but to keep moving once it was over. Seems like nothing's been the same since that battling and ruination, even way out here. Seems like we're still blowed to pieces. I can read and write for the basics, enough to make myself useful on a barge or a wagon pull, which is what it come down to in the end. Me and my wife settled with the Collins-Pruitt Assembly near Danville for as long as that lasted. Have you heard of it? The Pillars was down that way first. Then one of Brother Amos's camps. Collins-Pruitt made up a strong outfit for a time, and we was all fed and organized and in agreement on the schooling of children. But it faltered when the fevers run through, like things do when men want more than they can get. Me and my wife decided to get closer to blood family at Snow Creek. They still grow tobacco down there when they got men enough to guard it. They got a cattle herd, too. Most things are done in cooperation around Snow Creek."

She nodded. She had traveled that direction once or twice. There were good weavers of cloth in that part of the country. And women who traded in herbs and dyes.

"I believe I'm talking too much," the man said, finally removing his hat. His narrow head was shaved in the manner of a penitent or one who had been peeled by grief. It was scarred, as well. Some of the scars were intentional, relics of Mr. Hendricks's military service. Others were not. She reckoned that he, like many she had met, had spent time in someone's prison.

"It's all right," she said. "Talk is how we get there. When you're ready with the particulars of your request, I'll be listening."

They were weeds of a similar kind, she thought, looking at him again with a sense of prickling beneath her collarbones. He in his rusted jacket, a garment of patched and mossy wool; she in her heavy greenish sweater, reknit with her own hands during hours when the shaking and numbness weren't too bad. Grizzled human weeds. Tough. Quick to find territory. Her own head had been kept shorn for many years. But she no longer feared the voices within her skull as much as she once had. Her hair, now trimmed with whatever blade she had on hand, was an uneven thicket of browns and grays.

"They say you take fair payment," the man said.

"I take what the work requires. There's no magic—"

"I ain't here to ask for magic," he interrupted. "I ain't a fool. But it's a power, I know it is. It's pure power what you do."

"I don't claim power," she said, resting her staff against the front steps of the house. She could hear wasps buzzing amid the shiny leaves of the boxwoods. Late-season wasps. Meat seekers. "Preachers are the ones with power," she said. "And the government, when it has a notion to roll these roads."

"Preachers make too many claims," the man said to her, disgusted. "I've heard them all. They ain't saved us from nothing. And I know you don't favor the government, not out here."

"Sit with me, Mr. Hendricks." She pointed to one of the porch swings she had refused to break into kindling. He was right. She would rather not discuss the government.

"Will you say where you come from?" he asked, seating himself on the slatted, squeaking swing. She could see his boots now, how good they were. And she could smell him better, the more private scents his body had stopped withholding. She waited for it—the musk of his weaknesses.

"I was born here," she said. "It's not very complicated, my story. I was raised in this house by parents who did what they could. The building is old, but the walls remain strong despite their sins and mine. The bricks come from clay dug right there near the road bridge. They were kiln fired by slaves long before I was born. The sills and floorboards were cut and milled by slaves, too. The history is far from happy."

"That kind of slave-keeping is done with," he said. "We fought till one side beat the other."

"Is that what you think, Mr. Hendricks? That slavery is behind us? Because I'm going to want to disagree. All we have to do is admit what we've seen with our own eyes. We could ask those people camped near the river for their opinion. Most of them have worn some kind of chain."

"I don't know what I think," the man said, locking his hands in front of him. "Not after all I seen. People been foul to one another as long as I been alive. They say there's something different here, though, a chance at healing. My wife was told that." He glanced down the porch steps toward the creek, the cold thread of water that had never been given a name.

"Your wife sounds good-hearted," she said. "And hopeful. I wish I shared her attitude. My father was a medical man, the first in his family to study that far in school. He did his kind of healing when there were simpler ways to treat our miseries. Things are different now. You might know what I mean."

He nodded. He said, "Did they try to burn you out? When people took to rampaging and stealing everything they could?"

"They tried," she said. "I can't tell you what stopped them."

They were both silent for a moment. The burdens of mistrust were heavy.

"I don't know what determines the actions of other people," she finished. "I've been surprised too many times. I can say there's credit laid at my feet that isn't due. The tasks I perform are simple. I don't work miracles."

"And the white stones piled over yonder, the curing folks say comes from them?"

"The stones are for my sister," she said, quietly. "She's dead. There's no denying the goodness and mercy she brought into the world. She *was* a miracle."

"I want you to write me a letter," the man said, staring into the gnarled cup of his hands. "Will you do it?"

What he wanted was the hardest thing. He wanted a letter in the declarative style, and he wanted to be with her—at least on the grounds of her property—while she wrote it. Then he wanted what they rarely requested anymore: he wanted her to memorize the letter before the pair of them destroyed it forever. He would cut and stack the wood before she began writing, if that was what she required. And he would camp by the creek, eating his own dried fruit and meat. He wouldn't impose on her. But he also wanted her to carry the letter to its destination. He wanted her to speak its words aloud in the presence of the person who needed to hear them most. He described the place she would have to go, where the letter would become his painful request for forgiveness. He had a name. It was a crossroads far away.

"You're asking beyond my limits," she told him. "I don't travel anymore."

Hendricks looked at her with eyes the color of shed snakeskin. She could hear some kind of emotion emulsify itself in the tube of his throat. He seemed desperate. "I got to do this," he said, gulping. "I got to make this right. I'll give whatever you ask. At Snow Creek, they tell that you walk all the way to Tennessee, or down to the lights of Richmond."

"I won't go to Richmond," she said. "I won't go there ever again."

"What'll you take?" he asked. "I ain't got gold or a living child. I got nothing precious left to trade."

She felt the old cruelty rise up in her as powerfully as a moon tide. Her sister had begged too, hadn't she? And begging hadn't saved her sister's life or gotten her what she wanted. Her sister had believed in the generous giving of gifts—valuables handed to other people willy-nilly and free of expectation—when she should have put her faith in the cold logic of exchange.

"There is one thing you could do for me," she said with the hard shape of her mouth. "It's a rare deed, something men around here claim they have accomplished when they're swapping lies. It won't be easy. You'll probably fail. But I won't carry your letter to that crossroads for anything less."

The days were growing shorter. Each morning was heavier with mist, slower to pour its thin light across the trailing hems of darkness. A killing frost would come soon. The ax would fall—and there was no way to know what the floods and snows of winter would cut from her this time. She told herself she had no reason to regret the difficult task she had given Mr. Hendricks. She had requested a risky thing of him, a feat of true value. And it was his own fault. He had pressed her. He had asked too much. She couldn't behave like a child, like a person who believed the bountiful years would soon return. She had a reputation to maintain, and a living to make. This was, as Billy Kingery had proclaimed, a small window time, an unpromised time of barter and trade. She must take advantage of it. Billy would make sure she paid a heavy price if he believed she was becoming weak.

She heard the children of the Uninvited begin their approach to the cairn before she saw them. The clamor of their tethered goats. The yapping of the small dogs they kept in camp despite the dogs' uselessness. She knew the child who played the red trumpet horn at the head of the procession the best. The women of the camp sometimes sent him to ask about the mussels they wished to pluck from the river, or the small rabbits they hoped to snare on her land. The child had told her his name was Estefan. Now and again he left a clutch of wildflowers on her porch, or a cloth filled with eggs. The dogs would let him do that.

Estefan, Estefan. He played his horn badly as he always did. Despite his enthusiasm, he didn't have a gift for music. There were three small girls with him this time, each dressed in peony layers of skirts. They were delivering offerings to the cairn that had been built in memory of her sister. An old woman followed them, veiled and praying. Estefan had told her once that all the old women who lived with the Uninvited were blind, that they had been struck sightless by the last of the priests and their sight would return only when the saints did. She knew better. Estefan's story was just that—a child's tale. The blind didn't last long in most settlements.

There was a time when the government would have arrived at her door to protest the seasonal haven she gave to the Uninvited. There was a time when her more permanent neighbors, such as they were, would have plotted a dark-time raid to rid her fields of strangers. No longer. The current government, as unstable as it was, seated far away in its crowded capital, produced only uneven rhythms of taxation and toll. It saved its rare messengers for announcements of bland triumph. And her neighbors had dwindled, culled by hard, uncertain circumstances. They were no longer insistently belligerent. Those who remained had not been able to refuse the charms of Billy Kingery or the temptations of a truce.

Estefan, Estefan. She wished he played his hymns with a decent tune. She also wished he were more beautiful because that was one trait she could still bear to appreciate in a child—unplanned beauty. But Estefan's life had been too deprived, too transient and shifting, for him to become a strong and handsome boy. It was enough that he had survived the fevers. He was the oldest child in the camp. Very few children his age remained alive anywhere in the country. Yet he was still capable of the kind of unfettered happiness she could barely recall from her own childhood. She saw it in the way he led the smaller girls. She heard it in his flawed and joyful noise. He was naturally affectionate, and on good days, some unshriveled part of her wanted to share that affection. The boy was a reminder that she hadn't entirely misplaced her feelings for other people. She raised a hand in case Estefan happened to glance her way, hoping she could imitate a cheerful wave. But he didn't look in her direction.

The procession, although it silenced the morning songbirds with its trompings and bleatings, ended quickly. The children and their animals soon dispersed, separating amid bouts of laughter. The Uninvited preferred to keep their celebrations brief. Her sister, had she been alive, would never have approved of such homage, not even something as genuine as a parade staged by children. After she began caring for the sick and the dying, the children stricken by wave after wave of fevers no one could cure, her sister had become pure humility. She deflected all attempts at honor and praise. She believed in only one thing: compassion. On a morning like this, had she lived to see it, she would have chided the children for even singing out her name.

She didn't see Hendricks for three full days. When he returned, it was with a bloody sling knotted across his back. He dropped the sling at her feet. It landed with a squelching sound.

"I done it," he said. It was just past dawn. The doves that nested above the springhouse had begun their mournful duet. She had been on the top floor of the house, with the last of the telescopes, continuing her sister's charts as well as she could. She noticed that only the ragged-ear rat catcher trailed Mr. Hendricks. It did so with a sly cast to its eyes.

"It weren't my best hunt," Hendricks continued, staring at her. "Not by a long shot. I prefer bear, which I know how to track. But you didn't ask for bear. What I got here is the creature's head and heart. The carcass is too big to bring in all at once."

She examined him as closely as she dared. The tendons in his neck stood out like stems. His fingers made crawling motions at the ends of his blackened hands. "You're well?"

"Except for my pride. It weren't the clean kill I hoped for. I had to scarper across them bluffs a lot longer than I wanted. And it gutted one of your dogs, the dirt-colored one, when it was cornered, so I hope you don't have no feelings about that. I need to drag out the rest before it tempts your neighbors."

"You saw them?" she asked. "You saw Altices?"

"I seen more sign of them than I wanted. They been watching me close. But I got your cat."

Her cat. A creature she had never even seen. She had only heard about it, how it had stolen goats from the Uninvited, how it had stalked Billy Kingery's bargain men while the bargain men were stalking deer. "I'll help you," she said.

"No, ma'am, you will not. That ain't in the contract." He turned on her with the flint spark of irritation in his eyes. She was glad to see it. Fractiousness was good. Quarreling was good. He couldn't be allowed to like her. "I'll ask if you got a skinning blade. It would make doing what I got to do easier."

"Did you use a pit?"

"I ain't inclined to discuss my methods," Hendricks said. "I'm gonna work on the pelt, if that's all right. You said you'd commence the letter writing once I brung in the creature's head. You promised."

"I did."

"Then a good morning to you."

She watched him descend the porch steps toward where he'd made a pilgrim's camp under a poplar tree. He was tired beyond tired. She could see it in the way he walked. Limping. Canted to the left. Hunting mountain cats was not a task for a single man. The animals were swift and intelligent and wary. Their hides were precious. She had always wanted a cat hide for a rug or a coat leather. Now she had one. Mr. Hendricks, she had to admit, had proved himself more than equal to his desire for a letter. At least for now.

She turned away from her visitor and took in the dregs of the autumn sky. She would miss the fawn bitch. It had been a brave, if undisciplined, companion. Gutted on the hunt—that was a worthy epitaph, one she had to admire. She hoped the bitch hadn't felt more pain than it deserved.

She drank the last of the cow's milk while she stood in the cool stone hutch of the springhouse. The milk had been brought to her two days before by the peddler Mr. Lyle Laprade, he of the green eyes and rattling handcart and uncertain schedule. She had traded undyed yarn and a small packet of sleeping leaves for the milk, and she had allowed herself only a few sips at a time, for she didn't know when or if she would see Lyle Laprade again. She let the final drops melt like goose grease across her tongue.

Then she walked to the road bridge. The camp of the Uninvited lay quilted across the river bottom. They had come earlier this year, and grown larger. She thought she had heard raised voices coming from the tattered lean-tos the night before, a bad sign. The Uninvited prided themselves on their cohesion. She placed her right hand on the intricate column of her sister's cairn, which was now almost as tall as she was. Its stones were jeweled with the prying wink of mica and perfumed in the yeasty scent of the late-season flowers left behind by the faithful. The cairn's design had, in recent years, become as formidable as the beliefs it anchored. She gripped the stones with her fingers and tried to pray for a better self. She asked her sister, as she often did, for the forgiveness that could never come.

It was a request she made each time she began a letter for a stranger. She wanted her sister to know she was trying, in her own reduced way, to help another person—despite how things had ended between them. Her sister would have welcomed someone like Mr. Hendricks to the brick house with open arms. Her sister had been the better person in all ways imaginable. She, on the other hand, was riven with hesitations. The letter she had promised to write for Mr. Hendricks was already weighing upon her. She hadn't truly believed he would kill a mountain cat. She'd been certain he wouldn't earn the right to her services. Now she was honor-bound to complete her end of the bargain, and the prospect disturbed her greatly. Something was not quite right about Mr. Hendricks. Despite his common, placid face, he was too competent, too able to glide his way into her world without a misstep. She didn't believe he was who he said he was. Yet so long as he kept his word, she had to keep hers.

She repeated the vow aloud, hoping to stiffen her resolve: "I will aid any man who is not false toward me." As she spoke, the crows that roosted among the sour branches of the walnut trees took flight against the sun, their black wings flapping like rags.

By the time Hendricks returned with the pelt of the mountain cat, she had stirred and thickened her inks. Hendricks had crafted a crude sled from wood and rope, and he had strapped his shoulders into a clever contraption of harness. There were three dogs with him now—the dubious rat catcher, the brindle sight hound that had long played second fiddle to the dead fawn bitch, and a new one, a lugging beagle mix of the kind Billy Kingery claimed to serve in his Sunday stews.

"I peeled it where it fell," Hendricks said to her, sweating into his words. "I don't know how y'all do around here, how you stake your claims. I seen two boys in the woods, watching me. You'd have to reckon they's thieves."

She nodded. "Altices," she said. "Or Boitnotts. One or the other. They tend to be brave in the short run."

"I don't got ammunition to waste on boys."

"You won't need weapons," she said. "They'll come with a proposition. Mr. Billy Kingery has taught them that much."

Hendricks leaned into the wet straps of his harness as if he counted on them to hold him upright. His hat had been pushed clear of his brow. "I was lucky. The hide come free of a piece. I'll thank you for the knife."

"I'm about to start your letter," she said, turning her gaze to the vagabond beagle, pinning it with her eyes. She had decided she wouldn't allow Mr. Hendricks to witness any sign of her doubt or uneasiness. "I just need to select the paper. You're certain about the start of it?"

He nodded his narrow head, his eyes wrinkled and closed. "I am."

"Can you tell it to me again, the first part?

He repeated his invocation, slowly, sonorously—with all the bitter syllables mortised into place. What a great mansion it is, she thought. What a stout and foolish mansion is the human heart.

"It'd please me to know you're writing it while I'm clearing my sign from them woods," he said.

"Agreed."

"You'll let me know when I can see it?"

"I will."

"Then I'm gonna spread this pelt in your springhouse to keep it cool, and I'm gonna go back up them steep hills. Am I to salvage the entrails? I done what I could to bucket the blood."

"Leave whatever you like for the neighbors," she said. "Or keep it for yourself. You've earned it."

He looked at her with his scraped gray stare. "I want to thank you for that offer, but I'm coming to believe you don't put much stock in gratitude. You ain't what I'd call a grateful person."

She held a hand toward the bedraggled rat catcher. The dog
sidled forward and wiped its muzzle against her fingers. "I'm careful, Mr. Hendricks," she said. "Perhaps even more careful than you
are. You came to me for relief. Maybe I seek the same thing. But
relief is the pearl without price in this place. Just wishing for it be-
comes a curse all its own."

The inks were ready. The pens were sharp. She had selected a mottled
paper, two large sheets. The paper was imported, acquired some
years before by methods she preferred not to recall. It remained
spicy with the resins of foreign trees, redolent of lands she would
never be able to visit. Her instruments were gathered in the parlor
where the plastered walls bristled with the hair of long-dead plow
horses. It seemed appropriate to compose Hendricks's letter in a
room that was commiserating and congregational and old.

But she couldn't help herself. She returned to the second floor
of the house, up the warped and squealing stairs, and looked for
Hendricks through the beseeching lenses of the telescope. There.
Heaving himself clear of the scratching cedars, leaning into the
knotted straps of his imperfect harness. He was clearly a strong
man—willful and efficient. The dogs were like planets to his sun.
And beyond them, just close enough to suggest the kind of mockery she expected, were two other figures. Boys.

She watched until they crossed the road that was now so
rarely traveled, even by vagrants. Her mother's mother had stood
by that road and watched lines of wagons roll west to Kentucky
and Tennessee, when there seemed to be no limit to the riches
the world might provide even to those who lived far from the sea.
Land—every man, woman, and child on those wagons believed
their heart's delight could be found on a black-treed square of land.
Now, no one trusted dreams of good fortune. That naïveté had

ended. And a harder law prevailed: take or be taken. When she met Hendricks and the boys near the loose plaits of her vegetable garden, the boys shaped their faces into marketplace masks meant to hide their nervousness and hunger. They carried walking sticks and small bundles on their backs. She knew the tallest. He was an Altice by birth. She had heard him called Bofrane. She didn't recognize the smaller one.

"I left portions behind," Hendricks said, gasping into the heat created by his own body. "What we talked about. But I have drawed in some company."

"It's all right," she said, looking at the forked muscle and bone that was trussed onto Hendricks's makeshift sled. "I'll talk to them. That's a good-sized cat you have there. It's bigger than I imagined it would be. Longer-legged. But it's not the murderous female they tell stories about, is it? The one that births kittens the size of stoats? What you've got there seems to be a male."

"I don't want to hear about no female," Hendricks said. "I done what was asked without committing foul trespass. I followed all your rules. You said to me you would write and deliver my letter if I brought you the skin of a mountain cat."

She turned away from him, reminding herself of her manners. "We should hang the meat. The camp people will want to smoke it."

"I don't need your help on that," he said. "You got . . . there's other things you promised to do."

"I've started the letter, Mr. Hendricks. It won't fade away."

"That ain't how it feels to me, if you'll beg my pardon. All things pass quick in this world. They go away quick. I seen everything I value go to fade. This is a last chance for me. You might need to hear me say that."

She nodded, feeling the smooth weight of her staff in her hands. "I know why you're whipping at me, Mr. Hendricks. You've met your end of the bargain, and haste is something you value. But I

need to deal with our hill merchants first." She looked witch-eyed
at the boys until the taller one raised his dirty hand to her, palm
open and clear.

"We come for . . . trade," the boy said. His hair was curly and
black, though not as black as the bodies of the flies that had begun
to swarm the nearby carcass. His eyes were a motley blue.

"Tell me your names," she said.

"Mr. Bofrane Altice," the tall one said. "With me is Tul. He's a
Boitnott on his daddy's side and my cousin."

"You're not making a claim on Mr. Hendricks's kill, are you?"

"No, ma'am. My daddy, Mr. Alton Altice, who's laid up sick
in bed, wanted me to stand for that. He ain't never had a mountain cat. He says we're owed. But my uncle sees it different. Uncle
Willem sent us down here to thank you for the blood and whatnot
your man left for us near the line."

"That's not all your uncle wants, though, is it?"

The young Altice, who had the toadstool complexion of the
undernourished, shook his shaggy head. "He remanded us to ask
for a cat claw or two, if you was willing. He . . . . he . . ."

"He's heard I don't truck in that kind of charm," she said, com-
pleting his request for him.

Both boys nodded. The smaller, silent one, Tul, couldn't keep
the gleam of salivation off his scabbed lips.

"The decision is Mr. Hendricks's," she said. "He's a stranger
here. A guest. And he killed the cat. The ruling will be his."

Hendricks looked at her. He'd pulled the sled while wearing
one of his smoke-colored shirts. The harness had stained its X shape
across the shirt's rough fabric. "Is that how it is here?" Hendricks
asked. "At Collins-Pruitt, we—"

"At most places, the boss man measures out punishment and
reward," she said. "But not here. Here, the decision belongs to him
who's earned it most."

The boys dropped their eyes as the adults struck bargain. Billy Kingery had taught them well.

"Then I say these young ones can have the claws from one fore-paw to take to their uncle or whoever. I ask only for some help scraping and salting the hide."

"Yes, sir," black-headed Bofrane said, clearly relieved. "And Tul will make you a song, too. He brung his instrument. He don't talk much, but he can play."

Hendricks smiled through the sweat on his flushed face, the first smile she had seen. "That's a fair offer in any part of the land," he said. "No thieving?"

"No thieving toward your person, sir," Bofrane said.

"And none toward this woman?"

The boy paused. Both he and his cousin drew themselves up into a posture. They held their walking sticks like muskets in their hands. "No thieving toward this house, sir. It ain't to be done. Everybody on the river knows that."

She watched him make his ablutions from her observation post on the second floor of the house. As he stripped to the waist, he un-covered ribs that circled as tight as new wagon springs. Stripped naked, he glowed with the pallor of a man who habitually shielded himself from the sun. The telescope magnified few surprises. His shoulders and thighs were signatured with tattoos. Prison time, in-deed. But he hadn't been mutilated. Both of his balls nested with apple ripeness against the muscles of his thighs.

He would dry himself and dress in fresh clothes. He would stand at the foot of her garden and wait for her to call to him. And he would give his clean body to her if she asked because that was the way of it, the snare she could trigger, by right, at any time. It was an unwritten clause in their agreement. She recalled the smell of the animal he had killed for her: spoiled currant berries crushed with bone.

Mr. Gilpin, the dairy man, had never waited for her to call. He arrived with his cheeses and took her with the kind of rude, panting wrestle she came to enjoy. In the doorway of the house. On the hard slab of the kitchen hearth. Against the soil of her summer garden, both of them on their dirtied knees, moaning like curs. It had been midyear, the days dusty with pollen. Sultry. She could feel Mr. Gilpin's hands even now, callused, stained from hay stems, stinking of the silage he stored for the few spotted cows he retained. "I need at your woman's teats," he'd say, grinning around his wellkept teeth, and she'd lift the damp husk of her shirt to oblige. He could be gentle, lifting her breasts like hen's eggs, or he could be rough, twisting at her nipples, taunting her with the urgency of their mutual need. This was after the fraught, confused death of her sister. When it felt merciful to lie beneath a mere farmer, especially one who took such happy pride in his manhood. "I aim for us to feel good together," he'd say. "That's all it ever is." He came to the house as often as he could manage, never claiming to be a bachelor or a widower or uttering any type of lie he didn't believe. He wasn't stymied by the mysterious reputation of her sister or the strange faith that clung to her memory. "If other folks don't think the two of us are worth saving, then we're doing what we're made to do," he'd say, plunging thick inside her, causing her eyelids to feel as though they were rooted in flame.

He brought her molded cheeses and small pots of cream. She searched for his thumbprints in the cheese and licked at them with a kitten's greedy tongue.

Mr. Joshua Gilpin. There came a time when his visits simply stopped. Even Billy Kingery didn't seem to know the end to that story. Billy told her the dairy's spotted cows, as ropey and old as they were, had been seized by people claiming to be from the government.

"Josh couldn't provide no more calves for his contract. Some say he started humping them cows hisself in desperation. His last bull died or lost its seed or what have you. So he milked them girls until his fingers bled, but the milk wouldn't come no more. His only chance was to give it to them good with his own bull pole, but he still didn't get no miracle calves. Then the government moved in. Too bad for Josh Gilpin. All he knowed how to do was run a dairy with them spotted cows."

No, she thought, feeling not a single bloom of shame as she listened to Billy Kingery. That was a tattler's tale. There was plenty more Mr. Joshua Gilpin knew how to do.

Hendricks would come to her bed if she asked. He dared not refuse. But it wasn't what she wanted. Not now. Her examination of his body had brought the black serpents into her head. She lowered the telescope. The fingers of one hand were numb. They'd been tingling with familiar weakness for hours. No, now was not the time to feast on Mr. Hendricks. She would lay out fine sentences for him, instead. The ranks of syllables he had requested. The tidy brigades of words. She would write his letter for him while her palms still stank of brass.

"Is it like a sweet dream when you're writing things down?" her sister asked. "Do you feel like you're flying across the sky?"

She served his tea in a china cup, one that still had its companion saucer. They were the last pieces of her mother's cherished set. When the cup and saucer finally broke, she knew she would not feel sorrow. She predicted laughter instead—the laughter of the spurned.

"I'm sorry I kept you waiting," she said to Hendricks. "It falls on me sometimes, the making of sentences. And it's best if I stay close to the papers until the ink has dried."

"It's coming to you then," Hendricks said, trying not to gawk at the arrangements she had made inside her house. They were in the cluttered space she treated as her kitchen. There were bundles of roots and stalks hanging from the ceiling, and frames stretched with small animal skins angled against the walls. There were beakers and crocks and jars. "The letter's coming?"

"It is," she said, keeping her voice oriole bright. She didn't tell him she had taken a bath of her own, that she was—on his account—indulging herself in ways she hadn't allowed for longer than she could remember.

"I got to tell the truth. I ain't seen more than one or two letters of the kind you write in my whole life. There was a man at the port of Charleston who would scratch out your fortune on the leaf of a palm tree if you asked. He knew all manner of foreign alphabets. And I met a miner once who carved accounts of people's sins into the black rock of a mine shaft where nobody else could read them. You could pay him to do that. But it's new to me, asking something like this," he said, shifting uncomfortably in what she saw was a clean, long-tailed shirt. "I'll get at the wood chopping tomorrow. I reckon you have a ax."

"There's no need to hurry," she said. "This isn't a race between us."

He had no response to that.

The tea was her concoction—sweet grasses, rose hips, mint. There was honey from one of her sister's remaining hives, but neither of them spooned at it. She had asked him to sit in one of her square-backed chairs in front of an unlit cooking fire.

"The men from the camp are also cutting wood on my land. Sometimes they ask. Sometimes they don't. Use care."

"I don't reckon they'll mess with me if I'm working for you."

"Probably not," she said. "We have our agreements."

"You don't worry they'll pick you clean?" he asked. "It looks like there's more than a few of them set down in your fields."

"I've already been picked clean, Mr. Hendricks. Many times. Haven't you?"

He turned his face away from her then, his scrubbed and sun-drawn face.

"They're respectful," she told him, reminding herself to rest her cup on her knee so the palsy in her hand wouldn't show. "They keep the camp neat, and they're careful how much they hunt and fish. But they won't use the spring water up here. They won't even sip at it. They always boil water from the river, or the creek."

"That's just convenience," he said.

"I don't think so. They're somewhat afraid of me. No matter what I say or do."

"I'd guess everybody around here is somewhat afraid of you," he said, putting some volume into his voice. "I know I am."

She pretended she hadn't heard him. "They think if they drink from my spring water I'll steal from them," she continued. "And it's not their children I'll take, or their food, or their no-good metal money. It's their language. They think I'll thieve the survivors' talk right out of their mouths."

Hendricks sat dumbly before her, the small china cup nearly covered by his hands. One of his boots tapped against the floor at a jittery pace.

"They think my water will wash away the languages they share," she repeated.

"Will it?" he asked, his question sounding a little bleached.

"No," she said, irked. "Of course not. Unless I'm more of a demon than I admit, and I admit plenty."

Hendricks ran a nervous hand along the unshaved edges of his jaw. "Would you take it rude if I asked permission to step outside?"

She laughed, her teeth feeling wet against her lips. "You're not rude, Mr. Hendricks. I like your directness." She stood, preparing to escort him to more neutral ground. She could barely believe she'd considered taking him to bed. He wasn't worthy. "Please forgive me. I've forgotten how to be a proper hostess. My house and I haven't been lived in for a long time."

Outside, the air was layered with the scents of cooling bark and leaves. The sun flared behind the hill where the Hopkins house lay in ruins, nothing left to scratch at the sky but its four stout chimneys. Persimmons. The sunset was the color of persimmons. She reminded herself that she needed to walk to where the last of the tenant cabins still stood to see how the trees were bearing and if their late-season fruit was finally ripe.

"I'd like to say what I think." Hendricks had positioned himself at the very edge of her porch. He stood there no taller than she was. She could hear at least two of the dogs breathing beneath the boxwoods, waiting.

"Please," she said. "I've brought some of your tobacco. Let me hear you speak your mind."

He swung his shoulders in her direction, chin lifted. She held out a pipe, one she'd filled with a nest of cured leaves after she'd taken her bath. A surprise for Mr. Hendricks.

"Go ahead," she said, gesturing toward the pipe. "It was my father's."

He took it from her swiftly, as if it were already hot. He lit it with a flint from one of his pockets. She did the same with her own pipe. The new smoke felt dark in her mouth, unburied and dark.

He said, "I like seeing night fall among them people out there, the ones you call the Uninvited. That ain't a feeling I've had for a while."

"Is it the children?" she asked.

"Maybe. But that ain't the only thing that speaks to me. It's more the resting, the communing and the resting. I know there's bad people amongst them. There always is. But it don't matter, not when I can hear them settling. It's like they're building up for what might come next."

"They don't take more than they should," she said.

"That's only right," he said, clamping his teeth around the pipe stem. She wondered if he would leave marks with those teeth, just for her.

"My sister felt the need to care for people in the early camps," she said. "She tried to treat the fevers that somehow always caught up with everyone, no matter how far they ran."

"Is that what killed her, serving amongst the sick?"

"I'm not sure we have a proper name for what killed my sister, Mr. Hendricks. I haven't found one." She had become good at saying such things, at not admitting her own role in the matter.

He was silent for a time, sucking on the ghost ribbon of the tobacco. Then he said, "I been told she could raise the dead." He spoke in a tentative voice, as if he'd been afflicted by shyness. "That's what they say at Snow Creek."

"Then there are liars at Snow Creek," she said, "and I'm sorry you've met them."

"It ain't true?"

"You didn't come here for me to tell you what's true and not true, Mr. Hendricks. You came for a letter."

"Aye," he said, moving down the steps until he found room to sit by himself in the gathering gloom. "And I don't aim to cause trouble getting it. I apologize."

She said nothing. It was the tobacco, she thought. It never brought clarity to her thinking. Tobacco, even the finest of it, muffled her head.

"At Snow Creek, they'd think you was unusual for allowing them people to put down a camp," he said. "Folks worry the fevers will come back. I seen people make their own kin clear out at the first sign of sickness. At Snow Creek, they'd say you was brave."

"Then they are fools as well as liars," she replied. "Nothing I do qualifies as brave."

"There's a story they tell down there," he said. "It's one you might like, except for the end part of it."

"Are you a storyteller, Mr. Hendricks?"

"You know I ain't. You been writing out my letter. You, more than anybody, know just how pitiful I truly am."

"Tell it anyway," she said, sitting down in the best of the porch swings. "A story is a strong bridge across the night. And night is right in front of us." She knocked the wispy ash from her pipe bowl. The sound brought an urgent yelp from one of the dogs that had circled itself into sleep beneath the bushes. Guarding, she thought. Her dogs were always guarding things they didn't need or understand.

"It happened many years ago," he began. "Back when towns and settlements was even more isolated than they is now. A boy was born into a big family, a farming family that raised livestock and crops but made most of its living off tobacco of the kind we's smoking right here. He was a normal boy, or normal enough for his mama and his daddy. He growed up like he was supposed to, right to the age of seven or eight. He went to school part of the year, as did his many brothers and sisters, but the teacher made no remarks about him one way or the other. He didn't rise above.

"This was a churchgoing family. Or that's how it was told to me. But the preacher or deacon or whoever, he didn't have nothing to say about the boy neither. The child bore no kind of mark.

"It's said that one night the boy had a dream. When he woke from that dream, he rose from his pallet, made his way to the barn, and carved hisself a flute with his daddy's tools. And he commenced to playing an unknown music on that flute. He couldn't explain how it happened. He just all of a sudden took to making music, something he couldn't do before the dream."

"And no one said he'd been inhabited by a demon?"

"They must have. They knew of demons and those who claim to cast them out. But the boy didn't seem much different. He worked hard on the farm alongside the others. He weren't altered in any other way."

"Then he was a lucky boy," she said.

"Maybe he was, for a while," Hendricks replied. "But things changed. A man who'd been away from that place returned to it. The man was a sailor. He'd sailed on ships all over the world. Not long after he come back, there was some celebration or another— it must have been a wedding, that's how it was told to me—and there was liquor drinking and boasting and when a older brother asked the boy to play on his flute, he did so. Only this time, there was somebody who could sing to his music."

"The sailor could play also?"

"The sailor knowed enough to recognize the notes and put words to them. He said he'd heard the music before, on a small island far out in the sea. At Snow Creek, they tell that the sailor fell down on his knees in front of the boy in full surprise even though he weren't that drunk."

"It was a joke," she said. "A prank of some kind."

"It weren't," Hendricks said. "The boy and the sailor went at it. They made their music. They sang what they claimed were war songs, and love songs, and praiseful songs to other gods. Them who were present felt the full power of it. The hair stood up against their collars. Some who had been drinking even joined in."

"But that wasn't the end of it, was it?"

"No, ma'am. The next day was a Sunday, but many who'd been at the wedding stayed away from church and not just because they'd been laid low by whiskey. They wanted to be close to the boy, to hear what odd music he might play and to learn what the sailor might tell about it. Them people stayed all day and into the next night. The boy was bothered by the attention, he hadn't been seeking it, but he kept playing on that flute. He never sweat or got sullen or unskilled. By the time the sun set on the second day, some citizens was laying gifts at his feet."

"You're going to tell me the bad of it now, aren't you?" she said.

"I don't have to."

"You should finish. The finish is the point of such a story."

"I relay the end as it was told to me," he said, pausing to draw a great heave of smoke into his mouth. "Sometime on the second night, a person crept up on the sailor while he slept and killed him dead. Split his head with a rock. The boy was found dead, too. Strangled. The oldest of the boy's brothers admitted to the strangling. He was sentenced to hang for murder, but they couldn't find a hangman who would rope him up given the strangeness of the situation. And the brother denied any attack upon the sailor. He claimed he had nothing to do with it. He was pure fierce about that."

"And the flute?"

"Never seen again," he said.

"What do you make of such a story, Mr. Hendricks?" she asked, tasting the cavernous sour left in her mouth by the tobacco. "Why do your wife's people tell it?"

"I ain't sure what to make of it. I wonder where that flute got to. And I wonder why no man or woman admitted to killing the sailor. A decent person owns up to what he says and does. Why do my wife's people tell it? They tell it out of fear," he said, his voice becoming as thin as the evening air. "Fear's the reason behind most uproars in a small place. Them people could stand a odd thing that looked like a spell or a holiness as long as it was their odd thing, something birthed right before their eyes. But when it threatened to roam beyond them, when it looked like it might roll forward on independent wheels, then it become a danger. It had to be stopped."

He looked out into the gathered darkness, as if he hoped to see the edge of it. "Some people," he said, "them who connive the best, they know how to work that kind of fear. They like the strength you get from using it. And they like how it lets you do away with weak folks any time you want. Fear is a mighty tool for them that grip its handle." He paused once more, although he seemed to have finished the tobacco in his pipe. She realized, with welling discomfort, that she could no longer clearly distinguish the features of his face. The voice had become the man. And the man had more to say. "A fact like that ain't news to you," he continued. "You've paid a high price to survive in this world. I can see it on you. You're as thick-skinned and done-up and alone as anybody I ever met. You've learned to protect yourself from everything there is. I'm inclined to bet every word I said, all that I told about fear and the mastering of it, is a truth you grabbed hold of long ago."

She was angry. Sleepless. Throttled by her own bedsheets. How dare Hendricks speak to her that way. How dare he insinuate she was a manipulator of fear. He had no right to tell tales and wrap her in the meaning of those tales and expect her to finish his letter as if she hadn't recognized the wicked insult hidden among his words. No right at all.

After she had tossed and turned for more hours than she cared to count, she arose and climbed the protesting stairs of the house. The air in the second-floor rooms smelled of leaf mold and mice. Her sister's charts were more curled and stained and intimidating than ever. Ignoring them, she adjusted the telescope on its spindly stand with agitated impatience, but there were clouds over the moon she sought—fortresses and peninsulas of cloud—and she could see nothing. When she aimed the lenses toward the poplar tree where Hendricks was camped, she could see no sign of him either. Had he left? Was he sleeping without a fire? Was he heating himself with the cruel fancy he'd chosen to tell her? He had been baiting her with the story of the flute player and the sailor, she was sure of it. He had suspicions. He suspected the truth of what had happened to her sister, and he wanted to goad her into admitting what she had done. She wouldn't stand for it. Despite the deal they had struck with each other, she would order him off her land in the morning.

But when she returned downstairs to boil water for tea, something she hoped would calm her nerves, she was astonished to find one of her mother's ornamental lamps burning in the parlor. Its short, steady flame was no larger than her thumb, yet it cast an unstinting midday light across the entire room. Her nostrils, even from a distance, began to tingle from the peppery scent of her best ink. She looked down at her hands, afraid. But, no, her fingers were unstiff and unstained. She hadn't touched her pens or her inks since she had taken a bath earlier in the evening. She hadn't been near them. Still, the second sheet of paper she had chosen for Hendricks's letter was lying flat on the cherrywood table that served as her desk. It lay next to the sheet she had written on earlier in the day. The new paper was covered with fresh writing. Hendricks's material. Hendricks's confession. She could see that. She could read it for herself. Yet the letters linked across the page were as perfectly shaped as a schoolmarm's. The hand that had composed them was not hers.

The writing was her sister's.

She looked at the page twice, three times. She made herself read each sentence. But the evidence inscribed there didn't change, not one serif. Her sister? Her sister's handwriting? How could it be? Brimming with shock, she snatched at both sheets of paper and thrust them into the lamp's wavering flame until they began to burn. She held the withering, scorching sheets as long as she dared, watching the neat paragraphs shrink into oily ash with something like hatred in her heart. When it became impossible for her to breathe the smoke-scoured air swirling through the parlor, she covered her mouth and tucked herself backward into the front hallway, trying not to stagger. Surely, she would find Mr. Hendricks hunkered down in supplication or fraudulence on her front porch—waiting for her. The imposter writing must have come from him. He was engaged in an elaborate trick upon her. He was not to be trusted. And she would deal with him accordingly.

Except Hendricks wasn't on the porch, damn him. Only the three-colored beagle was there, tick-spotted and snoring. It took several swift kicks to rouse the unwanted animal and drive it from her door. But the dog's departure did nothing to lessen her panic. A message from her sister? It wasn't possible. Her sister had been dead for five years. Or was it ten? She sometimes had trouble remembering. Still, there had to be an explanation for the new page in Hendricks's letter. There had to be an answer. And she would find it. Even so, as much as she tried to steady herself with confidence and logic, she could not summon the courage to look toward the road bridge and the purposeful shape of her sister's white-stoned cairn.

She dressed meticulously in an attempt to waylay her fears. Stout shoes, woolen socks, her father's canvas trousers hemmed to match her height. It was still dark. She buttoned herself into a thick jacket and wrapped her left hand around her sturdy staff. This time, when she stepped out the door, she whistled for the dogs. And they came to her. The beagle, which seemed unfazed by her inconstant attitudes. The brindle sight hound. The rat catcher whose eyes shone as passionless as a fox's. And a new one—a bowlegged creature whose head resembled a white fist of bone. They had been close by. Surely they had not allowed Hendricks, or anyone else, into the house— a fact that troubled her even more.

"Come," she said. "We need to make a visit." And they strung themselves after her as she began a quick march toward the road.

She paused only briefly at the cairn, just long enough to perform a defiance she didn't truly feel. The cairn worried her. Just standing next to it made her heart feel the size of a pumpkin seed. "Don't mess with me, sister," she hissed, knocking at the bottom course of white stones with her staff. "I don't recommend you taunt me. You might not like the answers to the questions you've decided to ask."

The camp of the Uninvited, low-slung and half-planned, lay like beaten tin beneath the dented glow of the clouds. She ordered the dogs to wait near the road, and she walked toward the camp alone, humming, making noise, lest she be mistaken for a raider of some kind. As she approached the tangle of one of her own neglected hedges, she heard the thrash of something alive from within its branches. Her heartbeat pounced into her wrists. Hens, she told herself. It's not ghosts come to take you to hell; it's only roosting hens.

One of the younger men met her, a guard layered in mismatched shirts and armed with a slender knife. He was pale-skinned with the deep-set eyes and long teeth of those born on the shores of the great northern lakes. The fevers had been terrible there, terrible enough to drive entire towns south in search of solace or a cure.

"Council," she said. The man nodded. The Uninvited were patient with her requests. They were grateful she continued to welcome them on her land. The man led her expertly among the tents and scavenged awnings, finding paths where there seemed to be none, moving with both stealth and dignity. The camp was nearly quiet, but she could hear the slight coughing of children and the weary predawn murmur of adults. Roosters would begin to crow soon, and pigs would stir and grunt. She wondered where Estefan was. He didn't seem to have parents. She had never been able to tell who cared for him. She could have brought him a gift, something in exchange for the flowers and eggs he sometimes brought to her. If only she had been herself when she left the house. If only she hadn't been so . . . so disturbed.

"*Le conseil*," the man said in his northern language, pulling aside a heavy blanket. "The ones who speak for us today." He gestured that she should enter the featureless dark beyond. The council was always changing its location and membership, always hosting its petitioners in a different makeshift room. The Uninvited did not give authority to a single group of people for very long.

"*Buenas noches, mi perdita*," a soft voice said. "You have come to tell us something."

"I have," she said, trying to reckon her heartbeat with the sharp scent of burned sugar that filled the room. She was sorry the voice wasn't one she recognized. "Thank you for seeing me at this hour. I'm grateful. I have a visitor at the house, a stranger man, and he's been a bother to me."

"No, ooman," said another voice, this one deeper and smoother with its syllables, a male voice from the coastal islands where enormous plantations had once thrived. "The man's no bother. It's the journey that bothers. You must prepare for travel. Please sit to rest with us."

It was like this sometimes, the council acting only as a voice, or voices—speaking from where they couldn't be seen. She had dealt with them face-to-face before, many times. But she didn't get to choose when she saw them and when she didn't. Only the council chose.

"I'm not taking a journey, not a real one. There's a letter the man wants delivered. I said I would carry it for him. I'm supposed to speak it out loud in the place he once lived. I'm supposed to help him find forgiveness. But something . . . wrong . . . has occurred. Something I don't understand. I'm not going to make the trip."

"You travel already, friend," said a third voice, drier than the others, perhaps from age. "The long road is beneath your feet, whether you choose it or not. This is the way of all people. Let us call the boy. He brings you calm." Then she heard nothing more, not even whispering among those who were hidden from her, although she knew Estefan had been sent for. She flexed her shoulders under the weight of her coat, her heart ticking within her as loud as any clock.

"I'm here for advice about my hands," she said into the black space of the room, suddenly hoping to redirect the conversation. She had been wrong to come. It was foolish to ask the council about what she'd seen in her parlor. The Uninvited believed her sister was practically divine. They wouldn't understand why she was upset by interference with Hendricks's letter. They would consider communication from her sister a good sign, a blessing. "I've been drinking the marrow soup you recommended. Yet my hands continue to shake."

"Tssssst, friend," the third voice replied. "We won't talk about your hands today. You are here to find purpose. Sit."

She sat. The floor space was uneven with carpets. Closer to the ground, the air was even heavier with the torched scent of sugar, harder to breathe. Soon, a small figure tumbled through the blanketed doorway, half-awake, smelling of goat's milk and grass. Estefan. Smiling the smile of the drowsy. Not surprised to see her. He settled close, his trumpet cradled in his arms. She was pleased at how warm he felt.

"We have no news of your sister, ooman," said the second voice, the deep one from the islands. "There is no talk of her here, not for many days—although you think about her very much, and she is the reason you come to us this night. From us, there are the tributes to her only. And much gathering of food and wood for the winter. We are grateful to be your guests. We will not overstay our welcome."

She tried to place a palm on the woozy tangle of Estefan's head. Her whole body, not just her beleaguered hands, seemed on the verge of uncontrolled trembling. It was wise to be honest with the council. They had little tolerance for deceit. And they somehow knew what had actually driven her to see them. She began again. "I . . . I believe my sister has tried to frighten me. She has . . . interfered with the letter I'm writing for the man. She has written some part of it herself, and I can't . . . I don't understand why she would do that. I thought you might. You have always understood her. You have maintained the . . . the connection in ways I haven't. Can you tell me? Are you communicating with her? Does she want the man for herself?"

There was the sound of scratching—of claw on fabric—from behind the blankets. And a considerable delay. When the next voice came, it was the first one, breathy and soft. It sounded stilted, as if it had been coached. "That would be fair, wouldn't it, *mija*? You took something from your sister when she did not want it taken. The world seeks its balance."

She drove her eyes into the darkness, hoping she might see movement, the outline of a woman's jaw or a man's shoulder, something, anything that would give her an anchor. If only she could see a face. "I'd bring my sister back if I could," she said, feeling the boy nestled against her leg. "You must know that."

"Are you sure, friend? *We* would bring her back. All the Uninvited would see your sister alive again with gladness in their hearts." It was the third voice once more, sinewy and confident. "You mustn't fool yourself. You played a part in your sister's healing work. Then you stopped that work. Now your neighbors fill themselves with old wants. They are greedy and restless. They desire what you have and what you share with others. They do not like us. You must be ready for what comes next."

"Nothing needs to come next. I'll get rid of the man. He doesn't deserve his letter. And I'll maintain peace with the Altices. Willem is reasonable. I know how to bargain with him. My sister has been . . . gone for years. That's all I want, for things to stay as they are."

"You are mistaken," said the first voice, sighing. "Think about what you know, *mija*. Open your eyes. Remember your dreams. Your sister has never left you."

"Who takes care of this boy?" she asked, unnerved, not wanting to hear another syllable about her sister.

"Estefan makes his own prayers," said the second voice, fading below a whisper. "It's all a child can do."

"Are your men running patrols?" she asked. "Has there been sickness?"

But there were no more words. It was sometimes like that, as well. The council would close itself as tight and silent as a drawer.

Assurance. She'd been wrong to seek such a thing—especially from the contingent democracy of the Uninvited. No one deserved assurance these days, especially not her. She had posed a riddle to the council and been met with riddles in return. She got to her feet and stepped through the draped doorway into the smoky patina of dawn. Estefan followed, looking up at her with dulled and dreamy eyes. The bell of his trumpet was as inviting as the red throat of an enormous flower. In the past he'd been allowed to escort her through camp. He played new notes for her, leading the way. But this time he was quickly surrounded by those who waited for them both, silent men and women, their faces flat and careful and grim. Their chilled caution was as pervasive as their frowns.

"Estefan," she whispered as the boy was taken away before she was prepared to see him go. "Good-bye, Estefan." She watched him leave. She wanted to believe she had seen friendliness smeared across his face.

Only one old man remained behind, bent in the spine and nearly toothless. He bowed to her, as some of those who camped on her land did, before he turned on the flapping soles of his sandals. He clapped his hands together in a slow way that scuffed the hard skin of his palms as he walked in front of her, and the clapping—soft though it was—drew people to the doors of their piecemeal dwellings. Some of them joined in the clapping. Others didn't acknowledge her in any way save through the intense focus of their eyes.

When she was at the edge of the maze-like settlement, a woman stepped close, her thin hands curved into the shape of a bowl.

"Please," the woman said, reaching forward. "Please, just for you." It was bad luck to refuse a tribute, so she met the woman's fingers and grasped at the small bundle that lay there. The woman's face, she saw, was eroded with rivulets of grief. A mother, she thought. One of the thousands of former mothers.

"Thank you," she said, and the woman bowed so deeply it made her ashamed.

The dogs were waiting near the road, all four, their muscled backs sleek with dew. She didn't speak to them. She bypassed the cairn. She bypassed the thin scatter of Hendricks's camp as well. When she was up against the hard, brick hunch of her house, she unwrapped the bundle the woman had offered to her. Under a shroud of much-laundered cotton was a thong of bleached goatskin. Strung along the thong, separated by angry knots, were the skeletons of three locusts. The sight of those empty-eyed insect husks made her bones go cold. It had been years, but she would never forget the locusts and their maddening summer song. They had sawed and chirred and bred and died while so much was taken from the people who listened to them sing.

Three skeletons. Three children lost to the fevers. That was how she interpreted the gift. Was she being blessed by the woman from the camp, or cursed? She wasn't sure. She wrapped the locusts back into their cloth with shivering fingers. The council hadn't helped her. She couldn't blame them for not providing an explanation about her sister. Or offering counter charms or prayers or something she could pretend to believe in. The Uninvited had loved her sister fiercely when she had not. Why should they spare her now? That meant there was only one way to regain the solitude and equilibrium she craved. She would have to proceed with her plan. Despite the damage it would do to her reputation and her ability to scratch out a meager living, she would cut her ties to Mr. Hendricks. There would be no letter.

He was waiting inside the house. He had an oiled pistol stuck through his belt. Next to the pistol hung a long hunter's knife in a leather sheath. He was squatting on the floorboards of the front hallway, regarding the stairs to the second story as a forester might regard the bole of a great and dying tree.

"I beg pardon," he said, not even glancing her way. "I've took liberties."

"You have, Mr. Hendricks. You don't have permission to be in my house. You need to leave."

"Things has changed. I got something I want to show you."

"It's nothing I need to see," she said, starting to push past him. "I don't need or want anything from you."

"You don't hear it, do you?" His gaze remained upward. "I ain't surprised. My daddy always said I had the ears of a hound. I believe he was after your magnifier up yonder, your scope. I caught him quick as I could. He didn't have time to do no damage."

She made herself close and reopen her eyes while she slowly repeated his words to herself. An intruder? In her house? It couldn't be. Who would bother? This was another wild tale of Hendricks's, some infernal aspect of his planned invasion of her life. "Get out," she said, pounding at the words as if they were nails. "You're in breach of our agreement. You're a liar. I don't believe what's told to me by scofflaws."

"You needn't roar at me," he said, finally turning, his expression attentive but untroubled. "You'll find the boy in one of them rooms. He ain't been hurt much, though I did relieve him of his little hatchet. He's trussed up and waiting. I'll be in the yard, if that's your druther."

"Out," she said, the word feeling like a hard silver scale on her tongue.

"Yes, ma'am."

But it was as he described. She found the boy, Tul, tied hand and foot in one of her moldy upper rooms. He'd been writhing in the floor dust. His clothes were tarnished with it.

"Tul Boitnott," she said, breathing over him as she tried to sort through his possible motives. "There's them who cook and eat the children that tumble into their larders. You must know that. You must have heard the gossip about me."

The boy nodded, his brown eyes as wary as a turtle's.

"You should be afraid. Why are you here? I've been looted a dozen times. I have nothing but my papers and vellums and inks. You could ask for those, and I'd give them to you. I can't believe anyone in your family would have interest in my telescope. We've learned to leave each other alone. We have an understanding. What's induced this folly?"

The boy said nothing.

"I doubt you're the general of this army," she said, making herself think. "You must be looking for something else, something I don't have. Or you've been asked to create a disruption, to distract me. And there must be others helping you." She paused, reviewing all the oddities of the night. The boy's intrusion couldn't be related to the strange appearance of her sister's handwriting. That wasn't possible. But the council had warned her about her neighbors and their growing "wants." Both the Uninvited and the Altices were on edge for some reason. Newly agitated. All too stubborn. It wouldn't take much to tilt the balance of peace, and tilt it quickly. She would have to proceed carefully if she hoped to maintain the upper hand. "Even if you are a cowardly Boitnott, I doubt you'll speak freely to me. You'd rather take the consequences than tell who put you up to this. Am I right?"

The boy nodded for a second time.

"Then I'll have to make a tribunal with Mr. Hendricks," she said, scanning the boy's dirty face. His nostrils were rimmed with blood. "I'll call for judges among those who live in the bottomland," she continued. "The Uninvited will help me decide what to do with you." Her declaration produced a hard quiver across the bluish skin of the boy's neck. That simple sign was all she needed.

She descended the stairs feeling overburdened with weariness. She pressed open the heavy front door and called out for Hendricks. "The apologies are mine," she shouted. "I leapt to the wrong conclusions. You've done me a true favor."

Hendricks stepped from the purpled shadows of her yard. "There will be more of them," he said.

"Yes. My guess is young Bofrane is out there now. They've drummed up some kind of contest against us, or against me. Their families aren't honoring the pact. They fear the people in the river bottom more than they fear me, however. If Bofrane's wise, he'll try to make a deal with us before he has to tell his fermented daddy what's befallen Cousin Tul."

"We could hang that Tul from one of your high windows. It would be a sign to negotiate."

She looked at the man anew, considering the silent way he had emerged from the shadows and the air of menace that had emerged with him. "I don't war here. I never have."

"I don't mean hanged by the neck," Hendricks said, a stalker's gleam burning at the center of his eyes. "I ain't far gone enough to kill a child. I'd only strap him into a bundle, let him serve as a clear message. But have it your way. We'll wait for the older one to come to us. I hope he's too softened by your unwarring nature to go running to his kin. They want trouble. And there's more of them than there is of us."

They waited many hours. The dogs made their own haphazard survey of the day, racing against the bowlegged dog, snapping at flies, licking their sores and soft parts before they slunk under the bushes to sleep.

"The boy's rustling up his people," Hendricks said.

"Could be," she said, "but that would mean Billy Kingery is dead or has finally sold his authority across the counter of his store. Billy set the rules that keep the peace around here. We mostly abide by them. I haven't provoked the Altices, or anyone they're related to, not intentionally. But they want something. I need them to spell it out. My guess is young Bofrane will come to us with some kind of notion. In the meantime, will you tell me where you did your time in prison?"

Hendricks went as still as a perched hawk. "I won't."

"There's no shame in it," she said. "I served two hundred days in a place its colonel called Fishersville. I was very young."

"I ain't heard of Fishersville, and that's all I'll say on the matter. You aim to finish my letter today?"

She hesitated. She hadn't told him about her sister's handwriting or the visit to the council and how she had decided to cancel the contract for the letter. This was not the time to do so. It was an advantage to have someone with her, at least until the picayune raid by Tul Boitnott had been dealt with. "I believe so," she said, carefully.

"Then let's both think on that."

The boy, Bofrane, came to them as he had previously, from well across the road, although he showed a bow this time and a handful of fletched arrows. She called the dogs to her and let him be.

"We didn't mean nothing," the taller cousin said, slump-shouldered.

"You did," Hendricks said. "You meant pure invasion. Don't start your filthy begging by telling lies."

"Tul is all right," she told him. "Or as well as he can be. Say what you're here to say."

"My daddy, Mr. Alton Altice, wants reparation from you and your hunter man."

"Reparation for what? He got the cat claws he asked for."

"My uncle took those," the boy said. "Uncle Willem walked hisself off to Goggin's mill to make deals of his own. He didn't share with my daddy."

"So lazy Alton Altice has saddled up his high horse and put you on it," she said. "He thinks he's deserving? He wants more from me?"

"He says them camp people get everything they ask for and he don't get nothing. He says their men cross into his woods, stealing timber and turkey birds. He says they brung sickness to my aunt's new baby."

"That's not true," she said, taking a step toward the scabbed and dirty child, her staff tight in her hands. "There is *no* sickness."

The boy recoiled, arms raised around his head.

"I reckon it's possible you and Cousin Tul cooked up this fool stunt to avoid a beating from your daddy," Hendricks said, intervening. "He sounds like a unstinting bastard. But you're in thick now. You know what this lady can do to you?"

"She could kill Tul dead, I . . . I know that much," Bofrane said, his blue eyes dappled with fear. "And . . . and she could medical the skin right off my bones. They say she's learned the potions for that."

She squeezed her eyes shut and shook her head. No matter how accommodating she tried to be, those who lived around her never stopped accusing her of new horrors. Never. They knew what she'd done to her own sister. They knew she wasn't afraid to cross lines. "I'm not going to kill Tul," she said.

The boy rocked back on his heels with some relief. He was clad in a man's boots, cracked and big. "Then . . . then I request a honor swap. I want to take his place," he said.

"No need for it," Hendricks said, studying the black-haired boy with his hard gray eyes. "You tell your daddy he'll get no work from me, and he'll earn nothing but trouble if he keeps spreading talk of sickness and robbery. He needs to stop messing in business that ain't his. And if he beats on you for carrying my message, you tell him I'll hear it from down here, and I'll come for his pelt like I did with that mountain cat. Can you say that?"

"Yes, sir." The boy put a shape to his mouth that seemed both pleased and appalled.

"Then turn and walk yourself back across the road. I'll send your cousin out shortly. He thinks he's waiting for a tribunal from them you call the camp people. He'll be happy to see you."

The boy gulped. "You would have tribuned Tul?"

"We'll do what it takes to keep the Altice family from breeding criminals," Hendricks said. "You stay clear of this place."

"Yes, sir."

They watched as young Bofrane tried to retreat in his clumsy boots with some measure of dignity. The spotted beagle accompanied him for several nagging paces.

"It ain't over," Hendricks said.

"No, it's not."

"We got to finish our business right now. Can you write the rest of it while I stand guard?"

She hesitated once more. Hendricks had remained close to her the entire day. He had revealed a fine and patient way with the local troublemakers, and his skills might be useful to her again. He was also fiercely fixated on his letter. She was impressed by that. Perhaps she could produce some passable version of what she owed him. Quickly.

"Yes," she said. "I can."

"Do you need anything?"

"Only one thing," she said.

He looked at her from beneath the much-handled brim of his hat, preparing himself for another of her outrageous requests.

"Is Tul the one who makes music?" she asked.

"He is. He's fair good with a cut-down mandolin. He played while his cousin and me scraped the cat pelt."

"Then you'll want to be careful," she said. "The boy's fingers. Will you cut one off for me? At the knuckle?"

Hendricks continued to measure her without apparent judgment. His breathing was as steady as his gaze.

"I don't see how you can blame me," she said, looking into a sky bricked over with clouds. "We all have our wants."

She ate what she had: preserved tomatoes, unleavened bread, a handful of jerked meat. Then she stripped the upper half of her body, stood over her kitchen's cold cistern of water, and washed. Her hands felt strong and flagrant. There were no signs of palsy, not on this day. She wrapped herself in a tunic of retailored flannel. The letter. She knew just how she would make it sound. It would be longer this time, but more appealing, more flavored with the complexities of the man. It would be more like the Hendricks she had just witnessed.

Despite her plans to finish quickly, the writing went on into the night—and she felt no one's presence but her own. Nothing interfered with the work. She did not fret about the Altices or the council or her sister. She heard the patter of rain and the stony rumble of thunder. She smelled air-burned hints of lightning. But she paid little attention to the fitfulness of the atmosphere. She wrote so swiftly she used two full bottles of her richest ink and had to grind and mix powder for a third. Despite her haste, her brushes remained true, especially those tipped with human hair. She wrote without lamplight. She rarely paused. She thought she heard Hendricks circling the house on his patrols, sometimes castigating the dogs, sometimes singing his own guardian tunes, but she couldn't be sure. The declarations in her skull had become far more real than any connivance featuring Mr. Hendricks.

At some point she ascended the stairs and moved her sister's telescope to the northernmost window of the house. She put her eye to the crystal lenses and sought the notations of the midnight stars. In the one place the sky was clear, to the west, she looked for a brightness or a wheeling she might use within the letter. But she didn't go near her sister's dusty charts. She wanted no kind of conversation with her sibling.

When her hand began to cramp around the telescope's eyepiece, she beat the cramp flat against the knobs of her knees. And returned to writing.

When they were young, she and her sister traveled to the sea. She was transfixed by the water, struck dumb by its variable textures. To her, it looked like a living fabric, like a child's swirling skirt or a widow's long, dark veil. Her sister, however, was more haunted by the sky. "Do you see it?" her sister said, staring. "It's like its own continent up there. Mountains and islands, big blue canyons that never end. Do you see them? We could live in a place like that when we grow up, a country without people or a flag. We could stay there, just you and me."

"It's not like flying," she told her sister. "Taking their words from them is like diving. Writing for them is like diving into water, fast and blind and free."

She finished before sunrise. It was a good letter. She felt that in the burning of her palms. Yet writing it was only the start. She was famished but knew she wouldn't be able to swallow even a sip of stale water until she had read the letter aloud to Hendricks. He might reject it. They sometimes did. He might try to beat on her as if she were some false rag of a wife. She had borne beatings in the past. They were part of her price. And they changed nothing in the end. Not a single word.

She left the great sheets of paper, seven in all, laid out on the cherry desk, and she went to find him. Her legs were not as steady as she would have liked, so she breathed hard through her nostrils in an attempt to disperse the serpents still in her head, the long writhing alphabet of them. He had told her his transgressions, and she had recorded them to the best of her ability. But it wasn't safe or simple to take on the burdens of another person's history, all those sins and vacancies. The burdens sometimes stayed with her even after they were lifted from those who had earned them. They accumulated. So it must be. Translating human misdeeds was all she knew how to do. Her sister had been a healer and a meddler. She, herself, had nothing to offer the world except the recording of its failures.

There were signs Hendricks had been keeping vigil on her porch, but he wasn't there now. A torn square of tarpaulin lay crumpled near the doorstep. And she could smell the acrid spirit of burned tobacco. But except for the dripping of rain from the eaves of the house into the dark bowls of the boxwoods, she heard nothing.

He wouldn't be far. He had promised to watch over her.

She found him propped against the satiny trunk of a silver maple tree that stood near the road bridge. He held a naked knife blade in his right hand, and his head was pressed against the tree in such a way that his unshaven throat was treacherously exposed to the coming light of dawn. Her father's pipe was clenched between his teeth. She couldn't tell if he was dead or alive.

Her first instinct was to crouch low, to make a small target of herself. Her second was to speak to him, though only in a soldier's whisper. "Mr. Hendricks," she asked, "can you hear me?"

The implacable gray eyes, now filmed over with pain, opened. "I been hit good," he said.

She looked at his outstretched legs. The inconvenient sun was rising and lightening the sky, whether she wanted it to or not. She could see a shining tide of blood flowing from his left thigh into his lap.

"Arrow," he said, lips keyholed around the stem of the pipe. "Afraid I'd bleed out if I moved. But . . . I got the boy. At the garden."

"Bofrane?" she asked, crouching lower.

He tried to wag his head and failed. No. It was not Bofrane.

Tul Boitnott, she thought. Damn Tul Boitnott, as wicked as he was small. "We've got to get you inside," she said to Hendricks. "I'm going to lift you up."

Hendricks crabbed at her sleeve with the hand that didn't hold the knife. "Is it finished?" he asked.

"Your letter?" she said, trying to heft his weight upward. "Yes. But it doesn't matter right now."

"It's all . . . all that matters," he coughed, the pipe tumbling from his teeth. "I praise you for . . ."

"On your feet," she ordered, troubled by the quantity of blood that sluiced from the folds of his britches as she lifted him. "I'm not hauling you for praise."

He complied weakly, unsteadily, but with the kind of fixed

spirit she had come to expect. Hendricks would be a hard man to kill, she thought. She knew from listening to him that he was skilled at saving himself. It was no wonder he'd come to her for an absolving letter. He needed all the absolution he could get. As they hobbled up her steps, she was relieved not to hear any shouts or sounds of pursuit. The morning was thick with the moisture of the night's storm, yet the air remained strangely silent except for the constant rill of creek water over rock. Even the uncovered kitchens of the Uninvited were silent. No crowing from the roosters. No hungry bleating from the goats. It wasn't until she'd dragged Hendricks into the hallway of her misbegotten home that she thought to ask herself what had become of the dogs.

It came back to her as if she still did it every day, the melody and harmony of tending to someone who needed care. She kept rolls of boiled bandages on her shelves out of habit. And although she had sworn she would never watch over a sick child, not ever again, she wasn't about to turn away from a wounded man. Hendricks, stubborn cuss that he was, had pulled the arrow loose from his leg before she found him. She worked to stanch the bleeding while he held himself rigid beneath the pressure of her hands. He said he wouldn't accept any kind of tincture for the pain. They were coming, he told her. He had to remain alert. He had to make sure she was able to save herself and the letter.

"Who's coming?" she said, gathering whatever cloth she could find to soak up the blood. "Other than those idiot Altice boys, who wants to take us on? Who would dare?"

"You got . . . to understand," he said, gasping through the undulations of pain that washed over him. There was froth at the corners of his mouth. White froth. And his hands were shaking. He would vomit soon, and not for the last time.

"I understand blood loss and putrefaction," she said. "I understand coping with Altices. It's been done before. There's no one else to worry about."

"There is . . . another."

She sensed the convulsion before he did. She turned his head aside as gently as she could, allowing him to spew into a wad of flannel. She wiped his face, rebalanced him against the abused plaster of the wall, kept pressure on his wound. The arrow had struck bone. Hendricks was in for a lot of discomfort, but the artery had only been nicked. Her father would not have believed it—the nursing capabilities of his younger daughter, the fastidious, inward-looking child who shrank from messes of any kind.

She had water on to boil before Hendricks could speak again.

"Boy's dead," he told her, croaking from behind gritted teeth. "Too much . . . rain. Dark. Ambush . . . to ambush." She assessed the pale splotches on his cheeks and at the end of his hill country nose. Signs of heavy bleeding. The contents of his stomach were phlegm-like and soured. She could smell the stink of them above the hot iron scent of his blood.

"I'll tend to the boy," she said, barely meaning it. "But not until I have you right."

"S-sorry," he said, panting against a second assault of nausea. "Sorry for what . . . I done. A-all of it. There's things . . . going on. The b-boy weren't part of the plan."

He needed marrow tea. And rest. And careful cleansing. But she didn't sense the black-winged plunge toward death. He would survive. Tul Boitnott, she thought again, what did you start? And why? Hendricks was right. If the boy Tul was dead, they were in trouble. The Altices would harangue and threaten until they worked themselves into an irreversible fury. Unless Billy Kingery intervened to offer some kind of high-priced protection, they would have to barricade themselves against the entire clan. Or slip away while they could.

"I need you to drink some hot water to replace the volume of your blood," she told him. "Then you can witness the surgeon in me." He didn't even nod. She used a spoon to give him water, but it wasn't long before he passed into a spasming unconsciousness that allowed her, finally, to smear some poppy paste onto his lathered tongue. She cut his britches away from his leg, irrigated the puncture, probed it for metal and wood, and irrigated it again. Then she sewed it closed to the best of her ability with a curved needle that once belonged to her father. Hendricks's blood welled over her working fingers, slick and warm, until the very end.

When she had strapped the thigh with bandages, an aching relief rolled along the spindle of her neck. She grasped Hendricks's long-bladed knife from where it had fallen from his fingers and wiped it on her sleeve. Her hands and forearms were red. There were smears on her belly and large, spreading stains around her knees. Stirring in blood. She was stirring in blood again, a thing she had avoided for years. Ever since her sister's death, she had kept to herself—all alone. She had protected herself by bartering the only gift she had, the ability to write letters on behalf of the guilty and possessed. And, still, blood had come. It had spilled itself on her and within her house, flowing and marking, flowing and staining. Blood led to vengeance, and vengeance, as she knew all too well, was impossible to manage.

She peeled the ruined clothes from her body. Half-naked and stooped with wariness, she began a slow circling of the house from the inside. Her lower windows were shuttered as they had been for years, but she peered through the slats where she could, and she listened. She heard the inane territorial boast of a cardinal bird. And the crows—they were engaged in their usual confabulation in the high branches of the walnut trees. It was not enough. This late in the morning she ought to hear the ring of axes in the woods or laughter from the riverbank as the children of the Uninvited cast nets for fish. The camp's silence made no sense. She needed to know what was happening. As she clawed through her cedar chest for clean clothing, she told herself it would not be wise to step outside. A reconnoiter would be dangerous. There was, however, the telescope.

There had once been several telescopes, back in a time she could barely remember. Her father had been a quiet man—even before war trimmed his vocabulary and his happiness. He was perceived by those who knew him to be a just soul, so his silence was taken as a sign of good character. Medical instruments were his first love. He filled a tall, glass-fronted cabinet with the forceps and augurs and bone saws he used in his work. He became a stargazer only after his exhausting service in one tragic army, then another; after the unfortunate loss of his wife left him with the care of two small daughters. He spent many widowed hours attempting to read the heavens that spiraled above him, a glass of homemade rye at his elbow. If he found anything other than companionable silence among the stars, he had not said so. Now only a single scope remained, a battered, brass-trimmed thing that featured four adjustable lenses. It was the sole household object her charity-minded sister had refused to trade or sell. Some human weaknesses, her sister said, are meant to be preserved.

The telescope didn't work well in daylight, but she knew how to maneuver the lenses until she could gain the blurred perspective of an artillery officer perched on a sunlit ridge. She scanned the road first, then the open hillside to the south. The meadow there was close to the border she shared with the Altices. Nothing. She used her own eyes to survey her garden and Hendricks's rudimentary camp. She could see a pair of crows pecking their way toward something that lay in the emaciated thicket of her corn patch. If Tul Boitnott was dead, she said to herself as she pulled all but one lens from the cylinder of the telescope and took aim at that spot of ground, then he was even smaller in death than she had imagined he would be.

As she brought the black bulb of a crow's head into focus, a curve of unexpected color caught her eye. She could see what might be the tousle of human hair and the underwing pallor of a child's wrist. But red? A curve of bright red? She wrenched the scope into yet another position as dread purled down her spine. This time, she was able see the boy, or at least the trumpet he carried with him wherever he went.

The sight of his empty, half-curled hand made her retch both bile and air.

Estefan. Her Estefan.

One . . . two . . . three . . . four. She forced herself to count and breathe before she looked through the telescope again—just to be sure. She cocked her good eye fearfully against the lens. It was him. Her Estefan. Indeed.

There was no decision. Untethered by caution or good judgment, she began to run—across her scratched, untended floors and down her wheezing stairs. She was aware of only one fact: it couldn't be true, it wasn't possible. Estefan had no reason to be on this side of the creek, near her garden. He could not be dead.

Yet even as she raced toward him, hoping he was alive, hoping she could save him, her mind began to wrap itself in thorns. How had competent Hendricks come into conflict with Estefan instead of Tul? How could he have made such a mistake? The boys were nothing alike. Tul was larger and moved with feral ease. Estefan was a sprite. Also, Estefan and the camp children would never attack Hendricks or anyone connected to her. Would they? As she threw open the door of the house, other cruel and tremulous notions began to occur to her. What if the council's warnings were coming true in the worst of all ways? What if the Uninvited, somehow stirred up by the Altices or others, had suddenly lost complete faith in her? Desperate, she looked toward the road bridge, right at her sister's cairn. What she saw there drew an icy thread of fear through her veins. The cairn, its pallid stones still gleaming from the night's rain, had been smashed to half its height. Atop the profane wreckage, impaled upon a sharpened stake, was the head of the bowlegged dog.

Later, she told it to him slowly, understanding he wouldn't consider Estefan's death a crime, not at first. He hadn't known the boy. He wasn't familiar with the Uninvited or their ways. She began with the strategic. There was a heaped bonfire at the edge of the tree line to the southeast, and it was burning right now, in the light of day. Altices—men and women, boys and girls—were tending the fire and sharing in its significance. In her western fields, the ones occupied by the Uninvited, several smaller fires were also burning—one near the damaged cairn. Those fires were being fed by restless, shifting knots of men, the most able bodies in the camp, all of whom were armed. She didn't tell him about the dog's severed head.

She had done two things before she awoke Hendricks. Brazen things. She had gone to Estefan, and when she understood he was irretrievably dead, she returned to the house and unpacked a length of green silk from the very bottom of her cedar chest. It was the final remnant of her sister's flimsy gowns. Because the boy looked utterly discarded in death and because she couldn't bear to contemplate the meaty gap of his throat, she brushed her numbed lips across his brow as she placed the red trumpet within the crook of his arm before she covered him.

Then, for just a little while, it was more than she could bear. Her knees weakened. Her heart careened against her lungs, choking off her air. And she found herself kneeling next to the boy, rocking to and fro, to and fro, while her mouth filled with the fragments of a song she tried to sing to him, music composed from her own terrible confusion.

O, I wish there was a sail to see . . .

She sang to navigate a path toward pain. To find the agony she knew she deserved. The piteous costs of love had to be somewhere ahead, not far away. They had to be.

A boat made just to carry me . . .

She was all too familiar with the unsympathetic void that filled her skin nearly every hour of every day. It was her echo chamber, the grotto of her doom. The boy with the red trumpet had offered her a few tuneless notes of hope, but he was gone. She had lost the capacity to feel grief, or much of anything, when she was young. It had been taken from her, removed as the yolk is removed from an egg, during her calamitous days in prison. Her sister's assassination had hollowed her even more. Yet she had always hoped it would return to her one day, the ability to suffer. She believed its absence, her lack of communion, made her more of a demon than any hex her ignorant neighbors believed she was capable of casting.

O, there ought to be a sail to see . . .

Even when she was able to stand again, she couldn't summon the courage to carry Estefan's body into the camp of the people who loved him most. She dared not face them. So she lifted him, the tumbled and flapping weight of him, and bore him across the narrow bridge to the ruined sprawl of the cairn. She left him there, at the foot of the doused white comet of stone, telling herself that the mothers and fathers who called themselves the Uninvited, those weary souls who were trying to knit themselves together into some kind of durable fabric, would not want her to take him any farther.

They will never forgive us for the death of the boy, she said to herself, rubbing her stinging eyes with her knuckles. They will never forgive me.

Then she stood on the porch in full view of all possible opponents and whistled for the dogs. She drew in only two—the scrap-eared rat catcher and the lumbering beagle. The rat catcher had been severely beaten. It would be blind in one eye if it managed to survive at all. The beagle appeared undisturbed, as always. There was no sign of the brindle sight hound.

"So we are hated in both directions," she told Hendricks as she tried to persuade him to fuel himself with broth. "That's how it reads to me. Whatever line of protection was drawn around this house is gone. I don't know if the Altices and the others were both roaming last night, looking for one another or for you or for any kind of trouble they could find. I don't know why he . . . why the boy was close to the house. The council said trouble was coming, but I didn't . . . I don't understand. Maybe Billy Kingery and his damn bargain men have riled people up for reasons they haven't shared with me. Maybe fair truces aren't meant to last anymore. It doesn't matter. You struck the mortal blow. You killed the . . . that boy." She paused to swallow past the dry noose that constricted her throat. "The Uninvited will see you as my man, which means we have offended our only ally."

Hendricks, whose eyes now glittered with pain, made as if to get to his feet. He seemed to be signaling to her that he would accept his fate at the hands of the Uninvited—alone. He didn't expect her to pay for his mistake. His staggerer's face told her so. But she wasn't interested in his sacrifice. "Stay put," she said. "I'm not giving you up. That doesn't accomplish anything. I know how to get you safely out of this house. We'll do it tonight."

"No," he said. "I ain't a sneak. And I can't . . . I can't walk yet besides."

She recognized the truth in that. He wouldn't get far on foot.

"You," he said, pointing at her with a wavering hand. "You go. And take my letter."

"Damn your letter," she said. "That's done with. It's done."

"It . . . ain't," he said, coughing once more. "Hear . . . hear me out."

It took him a while to lay out his plan. His leg was very swollen. And he remained weak. Fleeing would kill him sooner than an Altice hatchet blade, he told her. But she—she could leave. Those who sought revenge weren't seeking her.

"I asked you to notch off young Tul's finger. His Altice kin will count that against me," she said. "They'll want us both."

"You asked me to make the cut," Hendricks replied, one half of his mouth slanting into a wan smile. "I didn't comply. The boy's got all his digits, though . . . though I meant to end his life last night. And I may do it yet."

"I've got nowhere to go," she said.

"The letter," he repeated. "You'll . . . you deliver it. I need you to keep that promise."

She sensed it again, hanging in the smoke-spumed corners of her witch's kitchen, deepening along the pine planks of her floor. Pure, pooling desolation. For years she had vowed to stay here, whether they came to burn her or bury her or lift her onto some kind of imposter's bier. She had made the house, its crimes and mythologies, both her penance and her grave because that was the only atonement she could imagine. It wasn't her fate to minister to the open world as her sister had done. She had inscribed another destiny—to be the unsouled one, the rememberer. She could not leave this place.

"No. I won't go." She wouldn't look at him as she spoke.

"Then we die like . . . like rats in a den." He coughed. "Or worse."

"We'll die like we're meant to."

He didn't waste precious energy on dispute. He spat into one of his hands and wiped the excess on the ruin of his shirt. His eyes, she saw, were as frigid as winter stars. "Then you'll do two things for me . . . if that's how you'll have it. You'll lay out the loads for my pistol, so I can see . . . see what I got. And you'll read. You'll read me your coward's letter."

His damnable confidence—the way he continued to concoct his weaknesses into strengths—shifted her despair toward rage. She felt the flames of her frustrations and inadequacies begin to flicker across her cheeks. How dare he question the quality of her work? How dare he question her judgment, especially after all she'd done for him? "If that's your wish, Mr. Hendricks, I'll read you an entire history of cowardice, but it won't be mine." She strode into the white-walled parlor, wishing the whole swarm of Altices would fly at them right that minute, heckling, destroying. She didn't want to suffer a useless chorus of human talking before she died, especially not with this man. "I'll start it from here," she shouted, not caring if Hendricks could hear her properly or not.

"*At this time*," she recited from memory. "*At this time in the valley of the river they call the Blackwater . . .*" The words she had copied down hummed across her tongue. She didn't even have to look at the first of the heavily inked pages. She spoke and she spoke, hoping Hendricks felt as miserable and trapped in his final cocoon as she did in hers. She stopped only when she realized there was a loud pounding noise coming from the kitchen.

"Come here," Hendricks called. "You need to c-come where I can see your face."

She went to him, seething.

"Say . . . again?" he asked, his own face now strangely open in its shape, lifted at the same angle she had seen only that morning, against the silvery trunk of the maple tree.

She began once more, the sentences buzzing past her teeth on their particular wings. She was beginning to regret the spat. What a pair of jesters they were to be quarreling at such a time, she thought. What mad japes.

He stopped her, brow furrowed. "I . . . I know I'm dizzied. But you ain't speaking in a voice I recognize."

She clenched her eyes shut so she couldn't see him.

"I can't . . . I know my head's light," he continued. "I can't understand why you're talking in a voice that ain't yours."

She turned from him, looking up into the kitchen rafters at the bundled barks and flowers she would never have a chance to use. There would be no more letters, no more paper monuments or pleas crafted at the whims of others. The life she'd scrawled out for herself was about to be erased. "Mr. Hendricks, I've had all I can stand of human miscommunication for this day, or any other. I've tried to be patient. My voice is my voice. I'm sorry you no longer like the sound of it. You've told me you know how to read. I'll bring the pages to you. You can puzzle over them yourself."

"You . . . you misunderstand *me*," he said, trying once again to lever himself to his feet so he could face her. "I'm asking who's talking out of your mouth. Don't you hear it? Why is she asking me questions with your lips? What does she want me to say?"

She spun on her heel to reprimand him one last time. But a hot taste lashed across her tongue, a heedless flavoring of gunpowder and brine, and then it was as if all the bones had been yanked from her legs. She fell that quickly. There was no way to stop it, no way she could bargain or complain or control the collapse that overtook her. It felt as though something, or someone, had grabbed hold of her very soul and was kidnapping it, subduing it for aims of their own. How strange, she thought, as she plummeted down and down and down—feeling as though she was being pruned from her own agitated body. How strange it was to die without planning or worry. How swiftly the struggle turned to sleep.

He was there when she opened her eyes. But not with his hunter's knife or the pistol she'd never seen him use. His body was naked and glazed by the yellow flickering of a woodsman's rock-ringed fire. She, too, was naked. But she was painted more in shadow than in light.

And he was loving her, more craftily than Joshua Gilpin ever had, more carefully than the besotted colonel from the Fishersville prison could ever have imagined. He hovered over her, his gray eyes closed tight with need. Dark hair had grown long on his skull, and his beard was untended. He didn't seem wounded in any way, nor did she. But there was a new kind of cold in the air. She could feel it against her skin. Brittle cold. A cold devoid of the moisture that came from long, slow rivers and from rain. She couldn't tell where they were, in what settlement or region. She couldn't locate a horizon or a sky. But the cries she heard—the joyful beggings—those hailed straight from her own mouth as she clutched him into her again, again, again.

"What should we tell them?" her sister asked as they dug the last of the small graves. "Are we stealing their unhappiness? Or just their children?"

"This is what I know," he whispered, leaning close to her face with its dry lips and crusted eyelids. "I know you're strong. I know you want to live. You can make it out of this house if you'll trust me. I'll be right behind you. We can see this through."

She was lying in a nest of blankets on the flagstones of the hearth. The stones were warm, but there was no fire. There was only the remnant heat of the coals, deep and throbbing. The air smelled smoky in a trapped and mangered way. She tried to draw her arms up over her breasts, which, because of the dream, she was certain were bare. They weren't. She was dressed. And Hendricks was tending to her, a clay bowl filled with water in his hands. How long had she been laid out, she wondered. Who was she?

"They shot fire arrows through the windows upstairs," he said. "That's the stink you smell. I doused the fires and closed your shutters, so the problem's settled for now. But I'm afraid your spring-house has been raided. I seen Altices coming and going from that direction. I bet they've took that mountain cat skin you wanted. It seemed smart to leave them be."

"How . . . how long?"

"You been out more than a day. Night's coming on again. It's some powerful prayers or spells you keep around this place, at least in the minds of the people who live close by. They are reluctant to take us on."

She struggled to sit upright. "You . . . your leg?" she asked.

"Swelled up thick and not good in any way you'd recommend," he said, showing again the rare crook of a smile. "But it's my turn to nursemaid."

"I don't—" She tried to swallow the hot pool of spit that had gathered in her throat. "I can't tell wha—"

"There ain't much to explain," he said, interrupting. "She talked to me without halt, even when I asked her to slow down or stop because I could see the toll it took on you. And I figured some things on my own. I found your escape tunnel the night before last when I was doing patrols, before . . . before I killed that boy. I found where the tunnel comes out above the creek. So I know we can get you across the river. Which is what we need to do."

She felt like an icy-skinned observer as she reached out and touched first the clay bowl, then the hard, knobbed bones of his wrist. He felt real enough. More than she did.

"They might have emptied your springhouse," he continued. "But you been laying up provisions in a proper way. I found them in the cellar. She—the one who says she's your sister—give me all man-ner of directions about filling your sack and what you need to carry."

"I don't . . . I don't understand," she said.

"Me neither," he said. "Not all of it. The voice that come from in-side you is a good and practical voice. She told me how to poultice my wound, though she admitted she weren't as good at making poultices as you. She told me what to swallow to keep my pain down and my spirits up, however long that lasts. She claimed she spent part of the time you was asleep copying the pages of my letter into your head. She says she can't keep you safe no more, only you can do that, but she has got you prepared." He shifted the clay bowl to his other hand and lowered himself next to her with a sharp sigh. Moving his leg was excruciating for him. Yet he'd done it. For her. There was a wet cloth in the bowl. And the buttons on her shirt were partly un-buttoned. So he had touched her body. The thought unnerved her.

"S-Ss . . ." She could not form the name with her lips. "My s-sister has been talking to you?"

"Without pause," he said. "She's as flighty as you once she gets going."

"I d-don't believe—"

"You don't got to believe," he said, placing a careful hand on her shoulder. She took note of the soothing shades within his voice. "Just test yourself on the letter. See if you remember it. When you're ready."

She didn't need the test. The first time he mentioned it, she had known—somehow—that his letter was within her forever, sheathed in her skin, inscribed in her blood pulse.

"You need to cross the river," Hendricks told her. "No arguing about it. You got a chance to be safe, to survive this. I'll stay a day or two, hold them off with my share of smoke and noise by pretend-ing we're both in here. Your sister don't make guarantees, but she said I should follow you as soon as my damned leg is ready."

"And if I don't leave? If we don't?"

"She hinted at a outcome we won't like. The destruction of this house, I guess. Or that camp you like so much. She don't seem to be much for compromise."

"She's not," she said, hearing again the hateful chirr of locusts, thousands of summer locusts, in her ears.

"She also claimed . . ." Hendricks hesitated. "She claimed she'd see me killed if you don't leave here soon. I don't want to bring myself into it. The two of us ain't got a formal bond. My risks is my own. But your sister, she aims to be persuasive."

And she knows me too well. She knows what it will take to make me complete this trade. She looked down at her blue-veined wrists as if she expected to see finely forged shackles locked around them. Why couldn't her sister let her be? They both knew she wasn't worth saving. All she'd ever accomplished in her life was betrayal. And why did Hendricks have to be made part of it? That wasn't fair, how her sister was using him—a man she barely knew—to force her to act. "I don't want to do it. I don't. But I guess I have no choice." She dropped her chin so he couldn't see the angry, shameful tears burning in her eyes.

"Then we're agreed," he said, clearly relieved, setting the clay bowl on the hearth. "You'll take that cellar tunnel after dark. Them Altices won't even know you're gone."

"Mr. Hendricks." She bit at the unhelpful softness of her lip. "Why didn't she just leave us to the ending we earned here?"

He looked at her a long time then, searching. He seemed troubled by her question, as if the strange voice that had come from within her had asked more of him than he could deliver. Before he spoke, he reached over and touched her face, just at the corner of one damp eye, with the ends of his fingers. "I can't say," he answered, lowering his gaze to the floor so she could no longer see any sign of the struggle that seemed to be occurring behind his rainstorm eyes. "That's one part she didn't spell out for me."

She told him the story of the tunnel, as much as she knew of it. The foundation of the house had been built from river rock many, many years before. There were two cellars, one accessible from inside, one from out. Sometime during the furbishing of the house, when the stairs were being raised, someone had framed a small hidey-hole between the two cellars. Later, someone else had made it possible to crawl from that hole to the entrance of a crude, rock-lined tunnel.

"I don't know if it was masters or slaves or both," she told him. "I don't know if the traffic through there was driven by good or evil. Once we were born, my father sealed the whole thing off, against rodents and the like. My sister and I opened it up, although I don't know what we thought we'd use it for. Maybe we thought it would help during the quarantines. But the things that finally rained down on us couldn't be helped by a tunnel."

"And now it's there and waiting," he said. He was wiping his wood-handled pistol with his shirttail, weighing it once more in his restless hands. He'd told her he had ten reliable bullets. He didn't intend to waste a single one. "You can use it to get out of here."

"Maybe so," she said, once again feeling weak and useless at the knees.

She was provisioned and properly dressed. She had allowed herself to go upstairs one last time to see the crumbling, leak-pronged rooms where she and her sister had once slept in canopied beds like the undisturbed dolls they wanted to be. She laid a hand on the smeared brass of the telescope, no longer needing its lenses to measure the siege that surrounded them. The Altices had begun to run small, rowdy patrols along the far side of the road, sometimes lighting feeble, uncontained fires in the wet brush, sometimes not. Always, they shot a gun or two into the air, cursing as they did so. The men and women of the Uninvited weren't so careless. Estefan's body had been carried away, and guards had been stationed along the creek and the upper reaches of the road. The camp was battened down. Its occupants weren't interested in being on display.

Together, she and Hendricks had burned the seven pages of his letter, handling each sheet as if it were a billowing sail. She had pocketed her father's waggling compass. She told Hendricks she would use the roads she knew and take to the higher hills if she got into trouble. She had also, against all better judgment, promised to deliver his letter to its destination. It was the only chance she would have to see him again. She wanted that—to see him. He claimed he would follow her in no more than two days, although to what end neither of them knew. They didn't speak of a future.

"I owe a winter's worth of hardwood," he said, hobbling around the kitchen space they were using as their protected quarters. A broken-off hoe handle served as his cane. "I ain't forgot that."

"Neither have I," she said, feeling something grievously akin to laughter swell into her lungs. "You're in my debt."

Her statement seemed to draw the confidence right out of his lungs, to deflate him—and the invisible burdens he now appeared to carry so gingerly within him—to the point of actual pain. "I got many debts," he said, grimly. "I'm beholden to people who only care for theirselves. I want a chance to square things up with you when this is over. I swear."

"We're both survivors, Mr. Hendricks." She spoke gently, but with ballooning uneasiness. As much as she had come to like him, something was wrong between them. She could sense it in the rigid angles of his body. "You said so yourself."

"This time I mean to be more than a survivor. Can I hope my debt to you will shrink somewhat if I escape the local hooligans to find you? To be with you again?"

His words rifled between them, loud and true.

"Please," she said, moving away. She found she was having great difficulty standing close to him.

"Please what?"

"No more promises from you, or pantomimes. I can't bear it." She hadn't forgotten how his fingers felt against her face, how they moth-winged there.

He limped to her side more quickly than she was prepared for. He grasped her arm firmly in his hand and drew her against him. The weight and shape of his chest felt familiar to her in a way they should not have. They had only touched, after all, within her dreams. "I ain't miming. I want you to know how I feel and what I truly stand for before you hear things about me. Before you learn—"

"Stop," she said, shaking him off and facing her kitchen's battered wall. "We can't go down this path. You don't know what it was like for me during my two hundred days at Fishersville, in that prison. It's something you need to understand."

He exhaled in frustration, leaning on his makeshift cane. She knew he didn't want to hear any premonitions of capture or death. They had avoided talking about Estefan, about the curse of that mistake. For Hendricks, worry was a waste of time. But she could not let him declare any kind of feeling for her. It wasn't allowed.

She said, "I think it could give you an inkling . . . a kind of knowledge about me, before . . . before we say too much."

She turned in time to see his eyes drop toward the weapons, those precious weapons, that dangled from his belt. She felt a pang when his gaze left hers. His roving, changeable eyes had begun to remind her of the great sea that had once stolen her heart.

"I was young at the time," she said, "younger than you might imagine, and I was at the weekly market with my father. My mother died when we were very small. It was not a thing we talked about, but it became our father's habit to take one of us, my sister or me, with him to market when he went. It was my sister's turn, but for some reason . . . some poor excuse . . . she decided not to go. We used a simple oxcart to get to town. You'll remember. Horses and mules were rare enough after the war. They became even more rare later, done in by their diseases.

"I wandered the stalls while my father visited the apothecary and other suppliers. I greeted the vendors and pretended to test their wares. It's what I always did. The market was considered safe for those with the right heritage or connections. I wasn't beautiful, but on this one day, I must have stood out in some way. It's all I can figure, that I called attention to myself and, therefore, was seized. It may not have been true where you're from, but here the towns rotted from the inside. Men began to take what they wanted, anything they wanted, and call it law. My father never knew who his enemy was, but someone gave the nod that led to my arrest. Thievery was the first charge. I was wearing some jewelry at the time, small silver bangles I'd inherited from my mother. Whoring was the second charge. And that one was impossible to slip.

"The plan may have been to keep me in town, to have me serve as a hostage to some kind of politicking my father needed to understand. There would have been sense in that. My father was a medical man. He was useful, especially to those with power. But soon, whatever plans had been made for me were changed. I was carted off to an establishment that called itself Fishersville. A school for girls. A place for moral education.

"I've seen your scars, Mr. Hendricks. So I know you know the truth. I was shaved and branded, though with girls the brands are hidden in tender places. They didn't cut my hair because the colonel preferred his tresses."

She kept her eyes on him, testing. He would either flinch. Or he wouldn't.

"The details aren't important," she continued. "There were many girls at the school, some younger than I was. It might surprise you to know how rival it got, how tribal. But I doubt it. It's enough to say that rather than count the days, I gave myself over to climbing to the top of any heap of girls I could identify. If it could be traded, I traded it. If it could be sold, I sold it. And you must know that we had very . . . very little to make up our economy. Mostly only our bodies, and what we could do with them. It wasn't long before I was summoned by the colonel.

"You would know this man, Mr. Hendricks. He was large and boisterous around the mouth. Perfumed. He was unworthy of rank of any kind except among the far-flung and the craven. And he was a taster of children, of course. He had nothing but appetite for us, appetite and lies."

Hendricks had taken the weight off his leg by leaning against one of her heavy tables, and he was staring at her, nearly through her. He wasn't shocked. Nothing could shock a man with his history. But she could practically smell his sympathy.

"It was an . . . excessive performance," she told him, trying to keep the bravado in her voice. "Excessive in its aims and actions. Because I troubled the colonel in ways he hadn't expected. I knew how to read, which was a skill he admired, so he let me wander among his books. I was willing to mouth other languages to him, words I pried from those books, and that . . . that talent aroused the man. I couldn't sing, not well. And I was a failure at the naked dancing he was used to. But he fed me regularly and allowed me to clean myself, and I slept in a nook of my own when he had no use for me. There were other girls, many others. On occasion we were made to lie with him in pairs and triples. But that wasn't his greatest desire. His greatest desire was to have us one by one, to taste us until we tasted no more.

"I can't say why it happened, why the colonel lost himself the way he did. But he couldn't satisfy himself with me, not in any way. He tried. Hands, mouth, carved ivory, polished wood, open flame, every false wonder he knew. He tried cruelty and cooing. He struck me bloody. I did the same to him. But he couldn't scratch the itch. It was worse for the others, worse for the ones he called to him when he had failed with me. I covered my ears and felt pity for those girls more than I'd felt anything in my life."

"Stop," Hendricks whispered. "Stop what you're telling. I've heard all I need to hear."

She thought of what she was about to do, of the risky journey she was about to attempt, how ill-fated it felt, and how she was attempting it for only one reason that made sense to her—because *he* had asked her to.

"I'm sure you have," she said. "But there's no such thing as enough for some people. The colonel. My sister. Me. Some of us always overreach."

"That ain't the way it has to be," he said, drawing close again, standing over her with his assertive shadow, but not daring to touch her. He had become fierce again, as fierce and desperate as when she had first met him and he had begged her for a letter. "You just need to say the words I say. That your bad self is finished and done. That you made it through the terrible times, and the person you was is gone forever. That there's a future where you'll do better."

"I've tried," she said, speaking so carefully she could feel the sharp edges of her teeth. "Pretending forward doesn't seem to work so well for me. You mustn't think well of me, Mr. Hendricks. Please remember what I'm saying in case we . . . we should ever meet again. You mustn't care for me, or trust me. You can't. Whether I can trust you is another matter, one I'll have to cope with myself. I'll carry your letter to the crossroads you've described, and I'll speak it aloud, and maybe I'll wait for you. But I can't carry your goodwill. I was talented at frustrating the colonel. I stimulated him, he craved me, and I made a life out of my hellish gifts— at least for a while. The point is: for someone like me, someone who will do whatever she has to do, two hundred days in a place like Fishersville isn't very long. For me, you might say, two hundred days was only the beginning."

Body

Her sister said, "Do you remember the game we played against each other when we were small?"

She did not remember.

Their father taught them how to hunt ground moles with the bright tines of a pitchfork. He impaled the blind creatures as they dug their tunnels, watching the dirt pucker above the eager, toiling bodies before he struck, leaving the bloody, pink-nosed corpses underground as a warning to other moles. Although he was a man of few words, their father was decisive when he needed to be. Both sisters felt protected by him. Until the protection failed. She never blamed her father for what happened at the market, but he bore the weight of that failure for the rest of his life. When she was released from Fishersville, he welcomed her back into his home without hesitation, and she had hardly left it since. Now, here she was, paddling like a ground mole away from the house her family had pretended was a safe haven. At least no one was hunting her with a pitchfork. Not yet. All she had to survive was darkness and catacomb stink.

The tunnel that led from the house was long and damp and narrow. She wondered how Hendricks would manage it when the time came. He was thicker and bonier than she was; it would be a tight fit. Yet Hendricks seemed capable of every bold deed she could imagine. Invisible stones cut into her elbows as she thought about the strange, uneasy man she'd left behind. Who was he, really? And why had she dreamed about him so? Creatures she couldn't see stung her wrists as she crawled forward inch by inch, foot by foot. She mouthed her way past the probing roots of trees. She inhaled dry spores of rot. But she didn't slow down or stop. When she finally bellied free, gulping fresh air, there was no respite. She hadn't even gotten to her feet before she saw the terrible gift someone had left for her at the weed-covered entrance. Estefan's red trumpet. It was lying right there, surrounded by a circle of white stones pilfered from her sister's cairn.

You are not alone in this, the trumpet seemed to say. *You can't escape what you've done.*

Estefan's body—the one she had draped in silk—would be burned on a pyre before dawn, mourned and sung into smoke by people who now despised her. She should be there. An honorable woman would attend the boy's funeral.

But she was not an honorable woman. She never had been. As she reached out to touch the trumpet, she sensed the cold fog of the nearby river, its wallowing disinterest. She was alone once again, the state she preferred because it meant she could disappoint only herself. Yet maybe it would be right to take the boy's trumpet with her. Perhaps the council would bless her journey if she chose to bear a bright token of her responsibility. Perhaps it wouldn't. Perhaps blessings no longer existed. But what harm could come from carrying a memento from the boy? He had never failed her, or anyone. *You must prepare for what comes next*, the council had said. She felt as though she was prepared for nothing, nothing that could matter, but she placed the trumpet in the cloth sack she wore slung across her shoulders and left the accusatory stones where they lay, every one.

You must prepare.

She stood, uncertain and unshepherded, as memory of the

council's words grappled with the tangled shadows of the night. The truth was, the Uninvited had been right in one way. She was going to make a journey, just as they had predicted.

She knew the way to Billy Kingery's store as well as she knew the lines on her own face. She would go there first. She could cross the river and head west. That's what Hendricks had recommended— and it's what he believed she had agreed to do. But Hendricks was a habitual evader in ways she was not. It was folly, always folly, to sidestep Billy, especially if you'd torn a hole in his local spiderweb. He was the only remaining arbiter for miles and miles, the agreed-upon proprietor of peace. Even if the peace, such as it was, was quickly unraveling, it was necessary to pay tribute to Billy. After her sister's death, Billy chose to ignore her as long as she gave beans or corn to his bargain men whenever they asked. He appeared to take no interest in her letter writing. But she knew how treacherous he could be. She needed to make a deal with him. Otherwise, she would not be allowed to proceed.

The moon cast a weary watchman's light across the slanted roof of her house. A faltering wind nagged the grasses at her feet. She imagined Hendricks whispering to her, telling her to stay alert. She imagined his moist lips moving close to her waiting ear, nearly touching her. He had asked her to take care of herself. He wanted her to be safe. She could hear his rusty, unlatched voice waylaying her with his hopes. He had expressed them more than once.

Why couldn't she believe him? Why did his caring words rinse her in distrust even as they made her heart twist?

She shook her head to clear it, to gain some distance from the seductions of Mr. Hendricks, then eased her way toward a familiar tree line. She knew the terrain so well she needed only the soles of her feet to lead her across the tapestries of fallen leaves that lay upon the floor of the forest, yard upon yard of them washed silver by the parsimonious stars. From salty white oak to sweet mountain laurel to stinking stands of sumac, she worked herself toward the ragged border of what had once been her father's uppermost field. There were deer bedded in the shelter of the hickories. She sipped their ruffled scent. And wary hares, she felt them halt and quiver as she passed.

The surveyor's line at Mr. Poindexter's was still visible to someone who knew where to look for it. And a few apple trees remained in the Poindexters' orchard, although they had been thoroughly stripped by Altices and Billy Kingery's enterprising bargain men. The shapes of those trees were a welcome sight to her, nonetheless, open-armed as they were, as white-hemmed as acolytes. Mrs. Poindexter had died long ago. Mr. Poindexter, who had been a staunch widower, was highly valued for his ability to graft the branches of fruit trees one to another and to understand the trees' sulky moods. He had been among the last of the old farmers to lose his holdings to Billy Kingery before the uproar of the quarantines, primarily because he had no children and hadn't been able to bring himself to purchase an heir from someone else. That was how it went. You took care of your land or Billy took it from you. Your tenants disappeared or became loyal to some other farmer who had tillage to offer. Peddlers suddenly avoided your door. Your larder began to empty, leaving you with nothing but pride and crusts and scraps for your meals. Billy Kingery outmaneuvered.

The Poindexter place was nothing but a foundation now, a stone-toothed mouth yawning into a scattered sky. The house had been burned to the ground. When they were young, her sister had been fascinated by the Poindexters' piano instrument. She had desperately wanted to learn to play it. But Mrs. Poindexter died, and Mr. Poindexter smashed the piano to splinters in his grief.

Making her way past the ruins, she remembered as if from

a forgotten dream the first words she had ever heard about Billy Kingery. She and her sister were buying red apples from the Poindexters, back when coins and scrip were exchanged among people as easily as greetings. "That man," Mrs. Poindexter said, "is no better than the talking donkey in that story my granny used to tell. The donkey arrived at the rich man's barn from nowhere, and the rich man thought he would prosper from such a wondrous thing, but only woe came to the rich man and his entire family despite the donkey's ability to speak words and brag about its supposed powers. Billy Kingery is a donkey promise."

Beyond the Poindexter place was a strip of overgrown forest. Its ownership was in dispute, which meant Billy's bargain men used it however they wished. Then came the empty house that had witnessed the perverse starvation of the Willards, a family unwilling to sell to Billy. Beyond the Willards' place lay Billy's neatly tended roadside and province, for as far as the eye could see. She'd been told people had begun to fight with one another for the privilege of living close to Billy. They kept their houses whitewashed and repaired for him. They kept their livestock fat and available.

As she crossed onto Billy's side of the ridge, the castigations of a hoot owl rose from the Willards' broken roofline, and she heard prolonged animal scratching from the ditch alongside her. Fox prowl, she supposed. Or the idle scavenge of a pot-bellied raccoon. There were clouds west of the moon now, white-bottomed and smooth and unsullied. The clouds seemed to herald cleaner hours ahead. The very idea made her laugh.

The circle of queer barns Billy had built around the squat fortress of his store came into sight. The barns reminded her of the stumps of giant trees, sturdy and wide at the bottom, strangely aslant across the top. They had once been considered structures of promise and organization, storehouses for dried corn and beans, all manner of seeds and grains that people had agreed to share before the chaos of the quarantines. Now, the barns were admonitions of failure—unless you wore the shirtsleeves of a Kingery.

The scratching noise came from the ditch again, clumsy and salivating. She turned to face it, her staff held high in her hands. She also carried a bone-handled butcher's knife and a sharpened awl, and she reminded herself of that. Hendricks had armed her well.

But it was only the wandering beagle dog scrabbling onto the path. Mournful, tick mottled, so pleased to see her.

"I don't know what to say about a world that spares you and not the others," she said to the dog, both irritated and relieved. She nudged its muddy, hopeful ears away from her ankles. There was no reason to keep her voice down. Billy would already know she was nearby. "Did the council send you, too?" she asked. "Have you come to remind me of some other duty I don't understand? Because I'm not offering to protect you. If the man in that store wants to fry you for his breakfast, he can. He can fry me also. You need to understand that."

The dog panted, its tongue scalloped and lolling. The late lamented fawn bitch was the kind of companion she preferred. That speed. That consequential attitude. But the fawn bitch was dead. And here was its uninspiring substitute. Keeping the bitch's murderous jaw firmly in mind, she turned from the beagle and squared herself to face Billy's store.

There had been a brief time in her life when the walk to Kingery's Store was a reward. The very afternoons seemed to taste of confection as she skipped up the road on some errand for her father. Rock candy on a string. Black licorice that stained the tongue. Peanut brittle that galled the mouth with sweetness. She had never been afraid, or shy in any way. Other children had been. They didn't like the store. Mr. Kingery had a bad smell about him, her sister said. When their father reminded them it was poor manners to criticize a person's upkeep, her sister said the smell had nothing to do with upkeep. It came from deep inside.

Billy Kingery. He never seemed to age. There was never any change to the shape of his body, neither fat nor wasting away. His hair remained as smooth and lacquered as the lid of a snuffbox all the day long. He bought and sold every item you could imagine from within the confines of his store. He distributed homemade food-stuffs, celebrating the local sustenances as evidence of a history he announced as important and shared. It was why he ran a store in the first place, he said. To provide. To feed people just what they needed.

She nudged the building's wide, ill-fitting door open with a toe. She didn't have to stop the beagle. The dog didn't want to follow her. It settled onto its waddler's hips, prepared to wait. She had to admire its faith. It assumed she would emerge from the store the same way she went in.

The stale spices of indolence crept up her nose even before she crossed the threshold. Bread crumbs and dust. Empty bottles. Waxed paper stained with grease. The sated breath of a man who is com-fortable, content even, to wait like a dragon in its den.

"Well, I'll be," a voice said from its beetle-winged gloom. "It's the doctor's girl, the little woman from down the road who keeps to her pens and papers. I ain't seen you in forever. How you been?"

"I think you know how I've been, Billy," she said, trying to suss out the shadows, hoping there wasn't a smoke-shriveled bargain man in every corner. She didn't care for bargain men.

"I reckon I've heard a thing or two. Alton Altice is screaming banshee about the many ignominies he's witnessed from the throne of his drunkard's bed. He's charged you with too many crimes to count. He's claiming a long list of reparations. But I'd be paupered nine times over if I listened to squawkers like Alton Altice. Why don't you tell me what I need to know?"

"May I come in?" she asked.

"You're in," he said, laughing. "I only entertain them who choose to step inside."

She could see the parchment page of his white shirt and the filmy gleam of the counter he stood behind, its unctuous surface. "I have a man at my place."

"Well, lord a mercy, it's about time. Josh Gilpin won't come this way again."

"Not that kind of man," she said.

"Ain't no other kind," Billy said, blustering from behind a set of teeth she knew were as blanched and precise as his shirt. "You and me need to be straight on that. Josh Gilpin and you had a very friendly wraparound. You ever wonder why he departed from the neighborhood?"

She didn't take the bait. "This man came for a letter. Nothing more."

"You still in that business?" he said. "It's a waste of time if you ask me. My man Cundiff says you been swapping dyes and papers like a bank clerk when you feel like it. He says you put up a powerful garden, too—and sent me a proper share. You don't need to write out the words of some sad fool to earn your keep. I'll take them vellums you make any time. I can get a high price for them downriver. I'll trade you some nice things, too, things you'll like, just to keep you honest. And you won't have to scratch out the decorations of the alphabet neither."

"I'm as honest as I want to be," she said, assuming an upright posture meant to look more assertive than she felt. "The man came to me for a letter. I didn't turn him away, and it's not your business why or wherefore. We got crosswise with Alton when some of his young ones tried their hands at robbery."

"And damn Willem wasn't there to stop them," Billy said, his words suddenly guttural and low. "So I heard." She had gotten close enough to the counter to see Billy's hands. They were finely furred with short black hair, the gold ring on his right pinkie gleaming like an eagle's eye. "Damn Willem," Billy repeated, laughing again, but in an entirely different way. "I told him he needs to stick closer to home. Them boys is out of control. He needs to strangle that brother of his, or just take over, or both. I don't care which."

"My man killed one of the camp people living in my fields, a child," she said, carefully. "It was a mistake. Things got mixed up after that. I'm afraid rampage is what we're in for."

"We?"

"You know what I mean, Billy. Nobody's bringing this to your door. Whatever happens won't go beyond my lines. I'll sort it out."

"But you're *in* my door, darling. You're here. And I ain't seen you up this way in a very long time. That tells me something. Remember how you used to gambol in this direction when you still wore ribbons and skirts? You recall how trusting you was back then, all sunshine and desiring of sweets?"

She didn't answer. She wondered how Billy managed to make it seem as though the air in his store was wood-smoked, even stupefying, when there was no fire to be seen or heard.

"They're gonna kill your man, ain't they? One side or the other? And you want to save him."

"I'm not here to save anyone," she said with some effort. She couldn't afford to think of Hendricks, not even within the snail shell of her imagination. Billy would know. He would capitalize.

"You sure?" Billy angled the tip of his weaselish nose. He seemed to be jaunting behind his countertop, as if he were considering the first steps of a dance.

She nodded. "I'm not here about the families who are living in my fields either. I'm not asking your permission for that. Those people can stay as long as they like—and they can return whenever they want. I've made my decision."

She thought she saw his confidence narrow, just a hair. "So you ain't here for my protection? You're not looking for a loan of any kind? How about we play a hand of cards just to test your luck?

Some of us would like to wager on that house you live in and that ripe bottomland you lend to begging wanderers."

She shook her head. She knew what happened to those who played cards with Billy.

"Then what the hell are you here for?" he asked, flat-footed again. "Buying something? Selling? Please tell me you've come to make good use of my . . . what would you call it . . . my judgment. Don't tell me you're thinking of leaving Billy Kingery out of your plans?"

He was sparring with her, singing some kind of caged bird tune because he wanted to. Nobody left Billy out. It wasn't possible.

"Passage," she said. "I just want passage, the same way I used to get it. The man's letter needs to be delivered."

There was a pause then. She'd become fairly certain there were no bargain men in the store. Yet she felt surrounded. The shelves that laddered all four walls loomed over her, some full, some empty. Several of the large, misshapen bundles on those shelves appeared, from the corners of her eyes, to be moving. She also smelled the predatory tang of feral cats—the smaller kind.

"Blankenship," Billy shouted. "Get out here. Show yourself."

A tall man, as thin and notched as fence wire, emerged from some pocket of gloom. He wore overalls that were soft and white at the knees, and he moved without a sound. His face appeared not to feature the muscles of expression.

"What do we charge for passage nowadays?"

The man said nothing. But she could feel the fingers of his appraisal, all ten of them, probing every crevice of her body. He had the eyes of a timber rattler, unlidded and empty. When he was done, he gave his boss what appeared to be a dismissive shrug.

"Hell yes, you can go back to sieving the mash or what have you," Billy said. "I know you got better things to do. So do I. I just wanted to share this thigh-slapper with somebody. You used to have a sense of humor." They watched Blankenship leave the store, as boneless as cold wind. Then Billy turned back to her, be-mused. "That letter you're delivering is the last song from a dead man, if you ask me. Things has gone cattywampus at your place, and you're leaving? I didn't think you had the gumption to travel no more. This fella must've wormed his way in deep if he talked you into going on the road. He sweet on you?"

She tried not to blink. "I made a deal."

"Understood." Billy kept an eye on her as he lifted what looked like a crystal thimble to his lips. He spent a moment nuzzling the thimble, although he didn't sip from it. She couldn't say how the thimble had gotten into his fingers in the first place. "I made those rules. I know you got to honor the deal. But you don't know who you're working with, sunshine. You got no idea."

"His name is Hendricks. That's all I care to say."

"I *know* what his name is. I know everything about him. He showed up and laid out all his woes to you, didn't he? Confessed to many a crime? He's the kind of man I could put to good use, don't you think?"

She said nothing. She could not drag Hendricks into the ne-gotiation. Billy would either provide passage or he wouldn't. There was no use arguing.

"I bet he didn't tell you he'd been in these parts before. Back when I was getting started. Before your sister done me wrong."

"My sister never—"

"Hush up," he hissed, and she knew she'd begun to sail into the kind of dangerous waters she'd hoped to avoid. Billy Kingery never showed a temper. He claimed he didn't have one. "You shut your mouth. That sister of yours made me a promise. She said she'd mid-wife those twin babies of mine, and she didn't. She lied."

"My sister couldn't help your babies," she said, trying to reel her head back onto her shoulders, damn Billy Kingery for fogging up the atmosphere like he did. "Once she saw what was happening, once she understood that your wife—"

"She made a deal."

"No, she didn't. Because if she'd made a deal, you would have killed her for backing out of it, and that didn't happen. You don't tolerate trade breakers. Neither do I. My sister never lied to you. She told you she couldn't save your wife without losing those babies, and you didn't like what you heard."

"Maybe I was just waiting," Billy said, recovering himself with a series of short, sly breaths. "Maybe I knew you'd take care of her for me."

His words hurtled past her ears like panicked birds. This was not a conversation she could afford to have. Mrs. Poindexter had been right about Billy. He was a man for whom everyone else was a stepping-stone or a pelt. He had eliminated all rivals and partners, benefiting most when influence was handed to him merely because he was the tidy, smiling man ready to receive it. Billy Kingery had never been voted into office. He'd never lowered himself to go directly to war. He let others do his hard work for him. It was all about weakness with Billy and how he waited for men and women to lay their own undoing at his feet even before he asked for it. She knew she mustn't give in to him. But when she tried to turn away, she couldn't. The floor felt like wet sand beneath her, inescapable sucking sand.

"Your man Hendricks has sold women and children all his life," Billy said. "White, red, brown, black. He'll sell anybody. Did he tell you about the liquor he soaks in and the gangs he's led to riot? Did he tell you how he traded his most recent wife for almost nothing? That was less than a year ago."

It was better to walk into the maw of Billy's accusations than to run away from them. She tried her feet again. One step. Two steps toward the counter. Her staff should have been in her hands, but she couldn't feel it. It seemed to have disappeared.

"He didn't tell you about that, did he?" Billy said, regaining his preferred chortle. "He's had several."

"I'm only . . . I'm here for passage," she said, failing not to gasp. Her right hand had finally reached the greasy pane of the counter. It was holding her up.

"You'll get your passage," Billy said. "I ain't about to deny the girl who sucked my candy with her greedy little lips. But you'll have to do something for me first."

Here it was. The price that would dilute her blood to broth.

"Blankenship and me been cooking," he said. "We been having a grand time. There's apple butter. And squirrel gravy. And my granny's famous chow-chow. But I also been making one of my special meals. You'll have to sup."

She shook her head.

"You ain't got a choice," Billy said, levering over the counter toward her, his teeth as bleached as gravestones. "You taste from the bowl, then you get your deal. You and that Hendricks don't harm my men, and you don't touch my property. You got two days to get that letter where it's supposed to go, not a minute more. But you have to eat first."

She shook her head again.

"You're as stubborn as a murderer, I'll say that. No wonder your sister found the long end of that rope. I'm halfway inclined to admire how independent you are. But somebody needs to teach you a lesson about independence. It might as well be me."

He was gone before she could sift through her dizziness, disappearing behind thick curtains that led into another chamber she didn't want to imagine. Somewhere beyond those curtains was the place where Billy's kettles were said to roil day and night, sometimes filled with vegetables and meat, sometimes with things even the bargain men wouldn't talk about. Billy made liquor too. There were stills inside his barns. And barrels of whiskey stored under guard in caves above the river. But this wouldn't be whiskey on her lips. This would be a recipe meant to turn her inside out. It would be mischief and interference only. Maybe even poison. She had no choice. She had to taste.

"Just tell me which direction you're headed with that precious letter," Billy said, reappearing with a tray suspended between his downy hands. "South. East. Whatever. So I can spread my notifications. Then all you got to do is open your mouth and—" He burst into loud guffaws before he could finish.

"West," she said, nearly choking on the bile that was already fingering its way up her throat.

"Well, of course. West. More mercenary types over that way, and lots of rovers. You'll have to step light." Billy lowered the tray almost daintily. The rhythm of a fiddler's reel had returned to his conversation. She could hear the clogging in it. "No spoons, missy. I don't abide spoons. I like to keep things simple."

The container on the tray was shaped like a trough. It was miniature in size but as stained and crusted and lickspittle as anything found in a hog's pen. The steam that wafted from it was heavy and foul.

"Don't worry," Billy Kingery said, leaning close, snuffling near the bare skin of her neck until her toes shivered. "I promise there ain't no little trumpet boys in there. No cracked sister bones, either. You'll have to digest them meals all by your lonesome. I ain't saying you'll like what I've cooked for you. I'll be honest. You won't like it at all. If you get sick, well, maybe you can find some other man's sweet candy to suck on." He paused just long enough to show her the sleek, fat maggot of his tongue. "I'm within my rights to do this," he whispered. "You know the rules same as me. You've asked for a favor. You've also become a problem. You let foreign riffraff settle on your land. You irritate Alton Altice. You ain't keeping things quiet around that house of yours.

"I don't suffer problems for long. You got two days passage to get where you want to be, that's all I'm inclined to provide. I recommend you think about your lying bitch sister every step of the way. I still got a score to settle with her." He laughed across the crown of her head one last time. "I do thank you for the visit, though. You've plumb brightened up my day. Uncle Billy loves to tend his store. And he just *lives* to dish up what a body deserves."

Enclosure

There was a story her family had told for as long as she could remember, and the story was this:

Once, when a great war was in its darkest days, a soldier found himself riding through the countryside. The soldier was wounded or lost or had deserted his post. The tellings varied. He had nothing left to feed himself, but he stopped at a stream, needing water for his horse at the very least. He found a woman there. She was poor. The war had taken nearly everything she had.

The woman had heard the cannon for days. She wanted more than anything to avoid soldiers and what they did to one another. But she, too, needed water.

The soldier asked for help.

He said, "I am poorly, ma'am. I do not seek to trouble you in any way. But if you had bread for me, I would be grateful. A few crumbs only, to keep up my strength."

The woman felt she had no choice. She filled her bucket and led the soldier back to her hard-used home. Her husband had been gone for many months, fighting for the other side. She didn't know if he was alive or dead. The soldier didn't remind her of her husband. The soldier's accent was thick and foreign. And he was very, very young.

She had cornmeal and one last egg. She baked the soldier a johnnycake.

He said, "You have saved me with your kindness, ma'am. I want to repay you. I have few things of value left in this world. My honor and my horse are two of them. Please gather your children so I may show them a third."

The woman was afraid. She knew soldiers. She refused to gather her children. "I want nothing from you," she said.

The soldier insisted. He behaved as though he was in the last useful moments of his life. "Please," he said. "I mean no harm."

The woman's children, large and small, came in from the fields and the barn and the places they had been hiding. Their eyes were bright with wariness. They, too, had heard the cannon.

"I was brave once," the soldier said, weeping. "I served a great general with valor. He awarded me this gold coin. I have kept it ever since, never meaning to spend it at all. But it seems right to spend it now." And he slipped the coin from his waistcoat. It was delicate and flashing. Its surface was engraved with the general's long and famous name. The woman had never seen anything so rare.

"I leave it with you," the soldier said, getting to his feet. "There's no more valor in me. Feed yourselves as you've fed this stranger." After placing kisses upon the pale cheeks of the woman's daughters, he rode away.

But the woman did not spend the coin for much-needed food or seed or woolen cloth or news of her missing husband. She held onto it tight. At her death it went to her oldest child, who also passed it along, unspent. So it went from family member to family member. There was no valor in any of them. They had outlasted a war where brother fought against brother, where people had to choose a side. They never forgot that. What they invested in, instead, were the hard, forged links of memory.

Alphabet

She woke on a bare patch of ground. Her sack had been tossed nearby, torn open and emptied. The beagle was asleep in the splay of her legs.

The taste of Billy's stew hadn't killed her. But as she took stock of the weakness in her limbs and the bone-grinding ache in her skull, she understood Billy Kingery had had his way with her—as only he could. There was no food left in her sack. No knife or sharpened awl on her belt. All that remained was Estefan's red trumpet and a fiendish burning in her stomach that felt like it would never cool.

She rolled to her knees, too dizzy to do more. When she looked at the sky, it undulated above her, striped and wavy, as fragile as a mussel shell. Where was she? How long had she been there? Was there any chance she'd been left plundered in Altice territory, served up by Billy for that family's revenge?

There was every chance.

"Now would be a good time to offer me a magic carpet ride," she said to the dog.

Once she could stand, she stumbled ahead like a three-legged fly on the only road she could find. The beagle sometimes followed her, sometimes led. It seemed to know the way.

They saw no one. She knew that shouldn't be possible. The neat gates lining both sides of the road were latched. The fence boards were taut and tended. She thought she could hear, somewhere beyond arm's length, the solemn breathing of a burro. Families lived here. There should be laundering and the banging of pots. There should be calls and sighs and the tuneless whistling of those left to churn the butter. But the food Billy had fed to her—whatever it was—had somehow erased, or veiled, great parts of the living world. She could tell cattle had recently been driven along the route she followed. And the dog was insistent in its examination of a set of iron-sheathed wheel marks. The dog smelled settlement. They were passing through a village of wants and needs, but she'd been made blind to it. There was no one she could ask for help even though she was desperate for a swallow of water. When a trio of brown sparrows became brave enough to flutter into her path, she fought the urge to join them as they pecked invisible seeds from the dust.

The river couldn't come soon enough. The dog left her when its careening waters were finally in sight.

Yet the river was all wrong, too. It wasn't the river she recalled. There were no twig-chewing bargain men at the toll shed. No jostling herds of animals. No purveyors of dried fish or corn. No registered whores. Everything Billy Kingery made possible for his compliant community had disappeared.

The route across the river was open, however. The narrow wooden footbridge was swaying from its ropes. And the wayfaring beagle, tricolored and streaming, waited for her on the other side.

But the beagle hadn't used the footbridge.

You got two days passage. Don't hurt my men, don't touch my property. She could hear Billy's voice hissing like hot steam in her ears.

Hendricks, if he were present, would tell her to stride across the bridge as if she owned it, then reap the consequences. The voice of her sister would undoubtedly suggest she fly.

"I'm coming," she said to the dripping dog. She meant to shout the words, but they came out in a flensed whisper. The bridge wasn't a safe option. She'd have to remember how to swim.

She was unlacing her boots, hands hurried and fearful, when she heard the sound of a trumpet. Its uneven music came to her as a series of honks followed by a happy sputter.

"Estefan?" she said, tottering to her feet. "Has Billy Kingery killed me so well I don't even know it yet? Is my death prize that I get to hear you play again?" She was sure the sounds were coming from the murdered boy even though his red trumpet remained in the sack that lay beside her in the grass.

She peered across the minatory water, expecting to see the child on the other side. But it was only the mendicant dog. Squealing its impatient tune. Tossing its flop-eared head. The beagle was sending her a beagle message. Leaning over the current as far as she dared, she tried to see what it wanted her to see. And then she did. The half-hidden shape of a wooden canoe just downstream from where she stood, wrapped in shrubs and shadows. A canoe to carry her across.

"A boat's as good as a carpet," she said, still whispering. "Thank you, whoever you are."

She said to her sister, "Do you think we will become good mothers?"

Her sister said it depended on whether they nurtured the souls of falcons or of ants.

She toppled out of the canoe when it struck land and drank river water until her belly swelled. But nothing inside her cooled, not one degree. She knelt in the slick, oozing mud trying not to moan or keen. There was sweet watercress within reach. And spindly parsley root. But she didn't touch them. Billy Kingery had stolen her appetite along with her pride. Drinking from the river was all she could manage.

Her diligent, underspoken father had maintained a code when he journeyed for his work. He claimed that late arrival was often the test of a medical man—too late to help with the birth of a child, too late to halt the snake venom or the deadly bleeding caused by an ax. Yet her father never faltered. He tended to his patients even if it meant tending to their deaths. Care, he said, was a greater test than duty.

He cultivated the same attitude toward the vine rust that destroyed his blackberries and the years of drought that stopped the mayapple from blooming in the shade of his woods. He taught himself to withstand failure. Endurance has to be more than dignity, he told his daughters. You must have reasons to be strong.

But what were her reasons to be strong? Had she ever had any? With her sister turned spirit and Hendricks fading like the cry of a migrating flock in her ears, she'd been reduced to what? A lonely scribbler sustaining herself on the scraps of others' pain? Billy Kingery's slattern pawn? She told herself she had to keep moving. She couldn't allow Billy to thwart her so easily—even if she was unsure of her capabilities. She *would* deliver Hendricks's letter to the crossroads. That could be her goal and her revenge. If she earned any luck at all, she'd see the man Hendricks again, although what she would feel when she saw him she couldn't say. Billy's lies and bragging had confused her about many things, had turned her inside out in more ways than she could measure. Hendricks might fail her. Still, it felt right to go on.

Committed to putting one foot ahead of the other, she plunged her face into the water and drank again. When she felt what she assumed was a river pebble on her unhappy tongue, she spat into her hand and found a tooth in the middle of her palm instead. A child's tooth, hollow and ivory.

Her sister hadn't always been so serious. She had been engaged to a boy whose family dealt in tanned hides. The boy smelled of shoveled lime and, on some days, rinds of offal, yet he spoke very little and was willing to let her sister do as she pleased with the parts of himself he tucked into his britches.

But the boy died from a cough contracted during a rainy harvest. Her sister was stricken with grief. Their father also took the news poorly. He tried, but failed, to participate in the mournful funeral cortege with his usual poise. Friends described him as distracted and muttering and thin. He was, his daughters soon discovered, managing himself through his own final days.

Her sister brooded long and hard on both losses. She took up the private intricacies of their father's telescopes. She tended the most dominant of the hens. But she neglected everything else, especially her fragile, paroled sibling. This was new to the two of them: a spiritual rather than a physical separation. It did not go well. Before he closed his eyes for the last time, their father spoke severely, and incompletely, about what they owed to one another. It was terrible enough that his wife had succumbed to tumorous growths when the girls were small. Now he was leaving them too. He asked them to never relinquish sight of one another, not ever.

But the older sister crafted a private, iron-ribbed space that admitted no other person. She didn't attend to her sibling—or even acknowledge her bewilderment and pain. This self-willed exile lasted until the day one of the Saunders men, black-bearded and long-striding, arrived from beyond the surveyor's line at Bleak Hill to fetch medicine for an infant who was suffering from the fits. He didn't know the doctor of the house had passed away. The older sister answered the door with her usual pitying vacancy. Moments later, she donned an overcoat and gaiters and a large felt hat, ready to follow the Saunders man high into the hills to a cabin whose low-pitched roof was already laden with snow, their father's instrument bag gripped tight between her hands.

She woke in the shade of what had once been a barn. The sound in her head was not the sound of Mrs. Poindexter playing piano notes, not at all. It was the buzzing of flies, arrogant in their waistcoats of blue and green.

Her stomach felt as though it had become the pan for a clutch of roasting eggs. And something about Billy Kingery's trickery had caused her left eye to leak. Its stray salts runneled into the stagnant pond of her ear. Nevertheless, she believed she knew where she was. The walls of the nearby house were familiar. She recognized their height and pattern. The Kirkbrides, adherents to their own strict religion, bonneted, buttoned, awash in offspring, had lived there for many years. Admirable farmers, they had occasionally come to her father for advice, although only for the minor ailments their faith allowed someone other than their god to treat. They paid her father with quilted cloth and watch chains woven from their own hair. They sent sprigs of dried lavender to the women in his household. The Kirkbrides had been among the first to leave the region, before the fevers began their relentless spread across the hills and valleys. They somehow gleaned, through their own codes of prayer, that the sickness carrying off their horses and mules might soon begin to carry them.

She had scavenged the Kirkbride house when her sister was still alive, seeking wallpaper and bits of window dressing for their own use. Others had done the same. Some had left muddy boot prints and rude coils of excrement. Some had left more direct signs of despair—scorched stairwells and fist-sized holes in the walls.

And here she was now, unsure how she'd gotten to the Kirkbride farm from the river. She levered herself upright on her elbows, muscles quaking. The dirt she lay on seemed to understand its limits better than she understood hers.

Somewhere in a rodent maze of memory she recalled that she and the man Hendricks had agreed to meet each other again. But where? Was it the place where he'd grown up as a boy? Was it a disreputable roadhouse or a bustling public square? Her recollection, it seemed, had become as unreliable as her ailing body. She remembered Hendricks urging her to believe in him—despite his history of violence and double-dealings. He would meet her. He would slip between his enemies and find her. Hadn't he been a brigand all his life?

Two days. That was all she had. She remembered that much. The sun went upside down in her eyes when she tried to measure its implacable trajectory. Its light was fine and clean, ground sharp on the spinning grindstone of autumn, but she had no way to tell how much time had passed since she crossed the river in the wobbly canoe. She felt a fly tap at her lips with its pronged legs. It wanted to do its business in her mouth. She tried to find the strength to wave it away. She had sworn to meet the man Hendricks, but she couldn't remember why. Billy Kingery, that criminal of commerce, had given her only two days to make the journey. Then Billy had fed her something to slow her down. He might as well have hammered a ball and chain to her ankle, damn him for his false haggling. If she didn't find help, or a new body with stronger legs, she would never make it.

They began to bring their children, sick and not sick, to the fields below the house. They came from everywhere, even the quarantined towns.

In Hendricks's seven-page letter she had written this, just as he asked: *There is no harbor for the man who slays his kin, or next of kin. There is no fortress but the fortress of lies, which is constructed of empty breath and cannot survive true assault, for the man who puts himself above the sanctity of others.*

The last chapter of their trouble began when a very small girl arose from her sickbed, laughing and singing, if only for a little while.

The beagle dog turned into a boy. Or that's how it seemed to her. She was unsure of herself and very ill. When she tried to vomit, all that came forth was a wind that tasted of bats and their crowded caves. She found the boy napping next to the Kirkbrides' cistern where she had crawled in search of water. His round, bare belly was exposed to the sun in a posture the beagle preferred.

"You got to come this way," the boy said to her, gesturing. "I can take you where you need to be." He wore woolen trousers cinched tight with rope. He had serious gray eyes.

She knew the boy was right. The Kirkbride farm, what was left of it, was close to Goggin's mill. The mill would be cloudy with the hefting of harvested grains and corn. Billy's bargain men lunched and gambled and traded insults at the mill. If she took the road to the mill, she'd likely get no farther.

If she headed into the mountains, she might have a chance.

Her sister said, "We can offer comfort. We can shade their eyes from the sun. And bathe their bodies while we have clean water."

"But the children die," she argued. "They all die, no matter what we do. I don't know if I can bear it. We've been at it for weeks and weeks. I follow you. I imitate you every way I can. But I don't have your skill for failure. We haven't accomplished anything."

"We're providing care, and that's worth more than you know. You're helping me."

"They're calling it a miracle," she said, reminding her sister of the bind they now found themselves in. "One hour of relief for one little girl, and nobody wants to leave this place. They're saying you're a healer, the angel they've been waiting for. They plant themselves along the creek like pleading stalks of wheat. And they spread the word. If they stay, we'll be starved out. Overwhelmed. Don't you think they should obey the quarantine?"

The two of them had discovered the uncomfortable truth that one sister possessed what the other did not: beneficence, and a tolerance for helplessness. Neither of them was afraid of death. They had sat by too many cots and pallets for that. But the older sister liked to rock the cradle of fate. That was *her* comfort.

"I don't mean to trap you in what's important to me," she said. But she did. That's exactly what she meant.

Hendricks's letter also declared: *I have been made fat from the labors of others, from the kindnesses and charities of those who meant me no harm. I have often meant harm. I am carved from the rock of it.*

In the dream she is lying beneath an elm tree at the crossroads Hendricks has described to her, a place she's never seen. Her father knew it. The crossroads was a landmark during his travels, famous for its location near the headwaters of their river and for the towering pinnacle of granite that rose sharp and bare for all to see. It took more than a full day to ride there. The cattle paths and cart routes in the area were barely maintained. People didn't care to live close to one another that far up in the hills. And there were no maps. So the crossroads became a convenient meeting place for those who chose to meet. The government, her father was told, hanged accused traitors from the rock, brutal acts the natives never forgave or forgot. Tormented lovers had also leaped from those heights. Many times. Everybody knew those tales.

In the dream there is no fire, although she wants one. The roots of her teeth are cold. And there is no Hendricks, either, despite her plans and expectations. She is strangely hungry and can't help thinking of salt. The elm provides a huge bower, firm shelter from wind and rain. Somewhere within the amphitheater of her mind she knows elms are gone from the world. Toppled by fungus and blister, elms survive in the mountains no longer. But there is one here, bowing over her, also waiting.

The dream requires a strange propriety. Girls come to her in a line, one after another, in their crisp white dresses or peony-layered skirts. It is a kind of receiving line, without greetings or festivity. Without capering promise. The girls come and come. Their oval faces are stitched with solemnity, eyes closed like masks, mouths held bloodless and straight. Only one girl carries a letter. Its pages are clasped tight in her milky fingers. She looks like all of the other girls. It is up to her, the intruder resting in the importunate shadow of the elm, to take the letter.

She knows the letter is from Hendricks.

She reaches for it greedily.

When she opens it, the paper begins to burn.

"The government will come for us," she told her sister, peering through the shutters at the trammeled road that continued to present them with responsibility and turmoil. Families arrived day and night. They didn't ask for much. They believed their children could ward off fever by merely laying eyes on the humble, ministering saint who lived in the brick house. But they remained in the fields, hundreds of them. The younger sister had become so anxious her face was splotched with a rash. There were large, weeping sores on her arms. "They'll take us away because they haven't been able to save a single child. They can't allow even a hint of success to survive alongside their incompetence. People are leaving their homes. The government needs control."

She couldn't say what she wanted to say. That she was suffocating within the selfless atmosphere of her sister. That she had become afraid of who she would become if she was arrested and locked away again. Or even if she wasn't.

She woke in a hollow log. Thirsty. Encased. Sticky-tongued. A coffin, she thought, as panic clotted her lungs. Billy Kingery has tucked me alive in a coffin just like the colonel threatened to do when I sassed him. Her pulse began to clang like a bronze bell between her ears. Only the fingering of a breeze at her ankles kept her from shrieking out loud.

Maybe it wasn't a coffin after all.

With effort, she wriggled out feet first. She had no idea how she'd gotten inside the log. The last thing she remembered was walking a rocky path with the gray-eyed boy. Now it was dark. And there was no boy. No dog. The ache in her head had subsided into a dry, rattling sensation without rhythm or reward. Her belly, however, protruded heavily before her. Whatever was inside her remained hotter-than-blood hot. And it was growing.

No boy. No dog. A frigid light cloaked the trees that swiped at the sky above her. The moon was bruised with the tracks of animals she couldn't name. She guessed she was somewhere in the blue hills west of where she'd been born. How much time had passed?

She didn't know. She recalled she was supposed to be in a hurry to get somewhere, somewhere the man known as Billy Kingery didn't want her to go, but she couldn't remember why. Where was she now? Where should she be headed? It seemed that everyone, perhaps even Billy Kingery, had left her to fend for herself.

She squatted close to the nut-ripe loam beneath her feet, wrapping her belly with her hands, feeling it throb. She listened carefully to the sounds that coasted along the perturbed currents of the night. Then she heard them, the slow notes of a mountaineer's midnight hunt, the mournful hallooing of a pack of hounds on the scent. True hounds. These would not be the cast-off animals she'd learned to feed and curse and muster during her years alone at the brick house. These would be the canine servants of Billy's wastrel bargain men, creatures trained to be slavering and direct. Surely, they were searching for her.

"So that's it," she said aloud, somewhat uplifted by the sound of her own voice. "The time Billy Kingery gave me must be gone." Even in her woozy state, she didn't have to wonder why Billy's men were tracking her. She hadn't met the terms of her deal with Billy. That was the first fact. But a life, as Billy claimed, was also consequence deserved. And she was about to reap her consequences, every one. She couldn't deny that she had betrayed her very own sister, the person whom she was supposed to cherish and protect above all others, and she'd done it to save herself. Betrayals had to be accounted for on the almighty ledger. As did failed promises. Working her way to her feet, she sensed the larval shape of an additional regret wriggle deep within her body. What if she didn't get wherever she had been going? What if someone was waiting for her, someone who needed her? "I guess it's best to give the hounds a good run no matter what," she said, hefting the belly she knew would slow her down. "There's no reason to make it easy." She remembered a story she'd heard once, about a dog bitch that leaped gallantly, and fearlessly, to its death after it cornered a mountain cat. She would die like that bitch had.

"Are you watching me, sister?" she asked, raising her chin toward the unlidded sky. "Do you want it to end this way?"

"You're right," her sister said, rubbing her sunken eyes. "The government will come for us even though we haven't done anything wrong. The camp council says someone has reported us. Someone has told the government I'm calling myself a prophet. You know that's something I would never do."

Prophets become martyrs, she said to herself, *even when they don't choose to.*

"Don't stop them from taking me if it comes to that," her sister said, pacing their cluttered parlor. "You need to keep working if you can. You know what to do. It's the children who matter."

"You got to keep going." The gray-eyed boy was suddenly at her elbow again, smaller than before but very assured. He was dressed in country linens no more substantial than the mountain mist that had begun to rise from the damp and blackened ground. His face bore the same pallor as the moon's. "You left a good man in danger at your house," the boy said. "He needs your help. Don't you remember him?"

"Go on," she said, deciding the boy was a figment of her ruined, hopeful mind. She was keeping her ears tuned to the song of the hunting hounds. They were still at least one ridgeline away. "There's no reason for you to be here. I don't even recall how I know you or how I got here in the first place. All I know is my time is done."

"He needs you."

She turned to the child, exasperated. "Nobody needs me. I'm nothing more than live bait for Billy Kingery's bargain men. You might want to step clear. I have fast hounds to sport with."

"The log," the boy said with his colorless lips.

She looked at him again.

"The log. Get back in the log. Crawl up as far as you can go. And don't stop."

"Who are you?" she asked, feeling something spin like a wooden top inside her bulging belly.

"I don't know how to answer," he said, shrugging. "I would if I could. I like you."

"Into the log? Like a mouse into a snake hole? Look at me. I'm as swollen as a cow's udder, getting bigger by the minute thanks to Billy Kingery's foul magic. I won't fit."

The boy shook his shaggy head. "You got to keep going. It'll . . . there will be some hurt to it. Maybe blood. But there ain't no other way."

She stared at him as if he held the butcher's blade himself.

"Lean down here," the boy said, miming what he wanted her to do. "I know you want to quit. Your strength is dwindled. You think there ain't nothing to live for. But you got to trust me. There's a thing you promised to do, and you got to do it. Put your ear down here. Listen. I ain't fooling, I swear. The man you care about is calling your name."

At the prison called Fishersville, she was fed twice a day. Her morning meal was doled out by bull-shouldered women who spoke not a word as they boiled and flayed and hashed. There was sawdust in the porridge. Purse leather was fried as meat. Her evening meal, on the other hand, was personally scripted by the colonel who wrote it out in pen and ink on a fresh sheet of paper every day. He said he wanted her to appreciate preparation. He wanted her to know the pleasures of forethought and control.

It was a secret he shared only with her.

The high mountains were right before them, layered like purple leaves against a flattened, fading sky. They continued to work their way west, the direction she somehow understood she was supposed to travel even though she could not measure how quickly they were moving, nor how far they had to go. But she knew the slippery red clay of the fields that had once flourished under the care of the Kirkbrides and the Poindexters and the few Altices who had given themselves over to the plow had fallen far behind. She thought she could sense the icy headwaters of a familiar river. Perhaps her true destination did lie ahead. If so, it was a man's plaintive face that served as her guide, the brushing promise of its mouth, the way its gray eyes gazed into hers despite their many doubts.

The boy in the country linens was talkative. He said he'd been born in Carolina and hoped to return there someday. He was a good walker, far better than she was on the stony foothill paths given her condition. She remembered very little about how she'd gotten from the hollow log to here—wherever here might be— except the pain. The pain had been merciless. There wasn't enough left of her afterward to serve as any kind of compass. Only the boy kept her going. He chattered, and he took her arm when the trail was muddy or slant, and he didn't comment on the smells of blood and organ that wafted from her. He was learning to read, he told her. He wanted to memorize the names of the birds he found in his books. It seemed like information a man could use, all those names—and he intended to travel the whole wide world someday, he did. His mama had taught him how to tell the difference be- tween a bluebird and a bunting. Did she know such a thing?

"My mother loved buntings," she said to him. "She thought their color was better than any bit of sky."

The boy said he was learning his roots and herbs and berries, too. He was studying on them all. The red raspberries were better in Carolina, he told her. But the blackberries were sweeter in this country, if you knew where to find them.

"I can bring you some, if you want," he said. "It's past the season, but that won't stop me."

She shook her head. She still had no appetite. Her transformed body wasn't destined to eat ever again, although she didn't want to say that to the boy.

He prattled on, telling her a story about a fort in the swamplands that had been built from timber cut and nailed by women. He'd been told a fort like that could never fall.

"How . . . how far do we have . . . to go?" she asked, wishing she'd traveled more so the valleys and peaks of the mountains might be familiar to her.

"I ain't sure," he said. "The sun's ahead of us, so I know our direction's right. It can't be too hard to find the valley that river's in. The man we're looking for could be on the other side of the next hill."

"I don't really know the man you're talking about. Do you understand that? I have no arrangement with him." She paused again, sipping at the air, wondering how much more blood was likely to leak out of her, from between her sticky thighs. With her belly empty as it now was, it should have been easier to walk, but it wasn't. "I heard someone calling my name from that log like you said I would, or I think I did, but there isn't much that binds that man and me, maybe because I said so . . . so little to him, even when I had the chance."

"He knows the names of birds," the boy said.

"Birds? Maybe he does. He knows how to pay attention in the world. I saw that. But, with me, he cared only about his letter."

"Letter?" The boy acted as though the very word was new to him.

"Yes," she said, rubbing her fingers together almost fondly, despite the blood stippled between them. "I used to write letters. Just the way people wanted."

"They didn't write them on their own? To save theirselves time?"

"They didn't," she said. "They don't. It's not really about saving time. It's more about laying out the language of all you've done or failed to do, all you've said or failed to say, in front of another person. For a long time, I was that other person."

"And what are you now?"

"Tired," she said. "Finished. I feel very finished."

"Your man will be sad to hear that."

"Do you think so? Do you think a man like that can be sad? He got what he wanted. He has his letter. Or I have it, somewhere inside of me. I'm supposed to deliver it to a crossroads beneath a great rock where he wants to meet me. He knew someone there years ago. That person needs to hear his words, and I promised to speak them for him. I'm not sure why I'm doing it."

"Does it feel terrible or wrong?" the boy asked. "What you're doing?"

"I can't tell," she said. "It feels like it's the only choice I have."

The boy smiled one of his pondering smiles. "Maybe your man will fix you up when we get to him. There's been a lot of hurt to you after . . . after going through that log. More than I reckoned."

"Nobody needs to fix me up," she said, giving her own kind of smile. "I thank you for your concern."

"But you *want* to get to him, right? Maybe I was supposed to ask you that. Because it seems like he's mostly a good man. You like him. My mama used to say it's hard to be a good man. She said you had to work hard to stay ahead of the devil. Is that why you need to see your man? To stay ahead of the devil?"

"I can't . . . say." She felt something chilly and intricate, something like a fisherman's net, draw tight around her heart. "I'm walking in this direction because you told me to. That's all I can recall."

"Do you love him?" the boy asked.

"I . . . I don't know. If this is love, it doesn't feel like enough."

The boy rambled ahead, suddenly distracted, one hand over his brow to shade it from the setting sun. "I reckon we're close," he said, speaking as if he hadn't heard her at all. "He could be over that next hill."

"Don't let me stop," she said, calibrating the doomed numbness in her legs. "I'm getting weaker. Don't let me stop for anything. Please."

"I could carry your sack for you," he said, bright-eyed.

"You could," she said, gasping once more. "It's not heavy. I've only got this one thing inside it, a . . . a present . . . from a friend."

"What present?" the boy asked.

She barely noticed the slow, frigid caress that ribboned along the back of her neck. She was tired. So tired. "Just this," she said, shedding the frayed and dirty sack she'd carried from the start. "Look. You can see."

She was surprised how quickly the boy reached for the red trumpet, at his uncharacteristic greed.

It is almost the oldest story in the book: two children with the same parents, the older talented at one thing, the younger talented at another. The scale of good fortune should accommodate such a balance. Except siblings aren't weights on a scale. They are levers for envy. Thus, Cain murdered Abel and spent the rest of his days wandering a wilderness of his own making.

There was also the incident with Billy Kingery's youngest wife. There were many Kingery wives at the time. And their children had been strangely spared by the sicknesses. Some said the Kingerys were protected by their upright natures. Others said it was their secret diet. Nevertheless, the newest wife, a Redford girl brought all the way from Tidewater, requested a midwife for her lying-in. She was carrying twins. And although much of the news regarding the fevers was kept from her, she sensed the long-fingered possibility of trouble. She'd been raised with many superstitions in Tidewater.

By that time, children were dying in the womb. Her sister hadn't delivered a living baby in weeks. And it was best if the womb was encouraged to expel the dead child before true labor began. Otherwise, the mother fell prey to fever too.

The Redford girl wasn't given a choice. Nor was her midwife. Billy Kingery let it be known they must deliver the babies alive. The girl was courage itself, but the twins never took a single breath in the misery that was their mother's world. Billy Kingery, it was said, remained outside the girl's chamber until the last of her dying wails faded into the dawn.

She taught herself how to make new paper—bleached and clean—from what had been used by others. Grocer's accounts. Ledgers of animal husbandry. The bewildered scraps of clerks and guarantors. Her father's obscure books of surgery. She pulped the old pages and laid the new ones out to dry, like monstrous petals, on screens she framed with her own hands. She devised inks and traded for parchments. No one tried to stop her. She was home from Fishersville. The crime of her imprisonment was an embarrassment to them all.

Schooled in foreign languages. Tutored in depravities.

Everyone for miles, especially the scholarly types who introduced themselves to her father with the hope they could study her, marveled at how quickly she appeared to recover from her ordeal. They admired her handwriting and her silence. Curious and implicated, they began, one by one, to request surreptitious samples of her work.

My Love,

Your beauty is destined to outlast us all, as it will
outlast the diamond parade of the stars. Sine qua non.
Coeur de mon coeur. *Do me the favor of meeting me . . .*

Dear Sir:

All I request of you is calm. There is no better cure for arro-
gance than stillness. Please collect yourself, and consider. The
wagons of grain you sent east are safe with me as long as we
are able to reach a refreshed agreement . . .

Our Mother—

We miss you.
Please return home to us. You misunderstand.
We didn't mean the words we said. You mustn't believe our
cousin's lies . . .

They folded their papers, and slipped them into private pockets, and thought to themselves: she writes as well as a judge. Or better.

They came sooner than she expected. And there were only two of them—one man, one woman—both cloaked against the night. The constant chirr of locusts slipped through the doorway with them, that heartless anthem of insect breeding, that bitter reminder of the insensate business required to keep a species alive. Her predictions had come true. The government had decided to stop them. But what the government truly sought was procedure, not confrontation. It hoped to put a halt to gatherings like the one in their fields so families would resign themselves to the official camps, the sanctioned ones, where fortitude, rather than purported miracles, would maintain the legitimacy of those who pretended to be in charge.

"My sister hasn't purported anything," she said to the largest agent, a woman who stood wide-legged and pie-faced before them as though she'd been elected to her task.

The man said, "You wrote to say she calls herself a prophet, a savior. Remember? Remember your letter to us? You don't need to say more. Changing your claims might lead to your own arrest, and you don't want to go to prison again, do you? That's what you told us. You requested seclusion and control of your days alone— which we've promised—in exchange for your testimony. We've brought the supplies you asked for, the pigments and the parchments and the nibs."

"You are," the woman added, "an infamous criminal. Everyone will understand why you've done what you've done. It's to be expected."

But her sister didn't understand. She stood surrounded by those who had come to fetch her and the one who had bargained her away—she stood there in her frayed gown and exhausted modesty, and her eyes began to blaze with tears.

"What are you doing? What have you done? All we need with the children is more time. There will be a cure. There has to be."

"You told me not to stop them."

"And so you summoned them instead, as if they're a harmless summer tune? Have you forgotten what you mean to me, how you're all I have in my life? You're ending our work before it's finished."

"I . . . I . . ." For once, she could not find the words.

"Please," her sister said, dropping to her knees so she could embrace her traitor's rigid ankles. "Please take back what you've told them, what you've written. We can sort this out. I'm not ready for this to end. Give us—give me—more time."

But she didn't retract one syllable. In fact, she couldn't speak at all. Standing above her sister, she found she was able to measure the sharing and not sharing between the two of them more perfectly than ever. She could calibrate the jambs and lintels of unfairness and character and impulse that separated them, and would separate them forever. And she knew it would be useless to cry out that her sister was being taken away, that someone was arresting the only person who had healed anything at all.

For who would hear her cries above the ceaseless gnashing of the locusts that clung to the grasses and the trees? No one in the camp across the creek believed in her. They believed only in her sister. She was merely the woman who stooped next to her candles at night, recording, revising. Although she had bowed her head while parents groaned and wept, although she had cradled hundreds of listless children, they knew she wasn't truly one of them. While she harrowed the alphabet with her inks, they formed themselves in lines near the road bridge in order to touch the hem of her sister's garments as she passed. They burned the bodies of their children under the unblinking phases of the moon. They burned and burned and burned. Their faces were smeared with the terrible ash. Their tongues were sour with it.

"So it will be," her sister said, finally wiping her eyes and filling the curdled hush between them. "I accept this. It's . . . soon. I thought we had more time. I wanted you to care about them as much as I do. But I was selfish. I didn't take into account what happened to you in that place they called a school, the way you've learned to . . . distance things. Please don't second-guess your choice. When your conscience allows it, remember that I loved you."

And they departed. The body was not returned to the brick house above the creek, although the end was rumored to have been mercifully swift. A silken noose. A solemn drop.

She, herself, sat alone for a long time in the upper rooms of the house with the flinty eye of the family telescope trained directly upon her face.

Days later, an infant, child of those who would eventually caravan as the Uninvited, survived his fever.

From the letter she sometimes wrote to herself: *There is no weakness in understanding you are weak. Count the days that have been taken from you. Count them again. Then let them fly as birds unto the rocky shore.*

"Carolina boy, give it back to me, that trumpet. I'm not as final as I thought." She spoke through a fresh, surging pain in her belly.

"I don't think so," he said, swinging her sack as if it were nothing more than knot and thread. "That's not the plan."

"The plan is to walk to the crossroads in the mountains," she said. "We've agreed on that. You're leading me there."

"Plans change," he said.

"Who *are* you?" she asked, trying to steady herself on legs that were weaker by the moment. Her head was beginning to feel irreparably loose on her neck. "What's your name?"

"You learn slow," he said, looking at her with eyes as perforated as beads. "I know you're hurt, so I been trying to explain. I laid down the story as clear as skunk scent, but you still keep losing track. Maybe I should've talked about my family more. That might've helped. I could've said my mama was a fine woman who was handy with pie crusts. I could've said everybody cherished the way she sang a lullaby. Maybe you would've recognized me if I'd said all that, because you know about my mama. I told you about her when we first met at your house—how she couldn't stop the weeds that took root in her children, especially her oldest boy. How he left home early, that boy did, and when he come back after wandering up and down the country, he was much changed." The boy took a deep breath, then winked one of his disturbing eyes. She was most confused by his voice. It had begun to sound older to her. And familiar.

He continued. "The boy weren't entirely welcome when he come back to his family. His daddy wouldn't have nothing to do with him. The boy was said to drink and gamble. He was also known to be generous in his way, bringing silks to his sisters and a whale-tooth comb to his mama who was celebrated far and wide for the luster of her hair. But his mama never used that comb. She give it to her favorite preacher who ground it to dust under his heel instead. And his sisters burned the silks, which had taken him many months to earn, in a fire stoked by cow dung gathered by his daddy.

"The boy stayed near home for a while, a prisoner of the ties that bind. He began to make a name for hisself with dice and cards and his handsome manners. It weren't long before he was the beau of the prettiest girl around.

"But he carried pure destruction in his soul, the boy did, or that's what folks began to say about him. He took to gambling in bigger towns for higher stakes, sometimes losing but winning often enough to keep hisself in good clothes and liquor. He even took to wagering the woman he loved, unbeknownst to her. It was a terrible risk. He knew that. He felt the terror. But the lure of piled gold was greater than any fear. He lost the woman once or twice but he always won her back—her and more—before the night was through."

"Why are you telling me this?" she asked.

"Because you know what a boy, a man, like that does next," he said. "You wrote it in your letter. A man like that wagers the woman he loves and falls asleep drunk and wakes up to find his house empty and his woman gone, collected by another. He knows he's supposed to rage wild with grief and revenge, but he don't. Grief ain't at the heart of him."

"What's your name?" she said again. "I want to know it."

"You know my name," he said, his young mouth a dollop of pity. "You know who I am or, more rightly, what I'll turn into when I'm fully growed. You put my story down on your precious paper hoping it would do me some good to have it all laid out, admission after admission, sin up against sin, wrong linked to wrong. But I can't be changed much by what's on a piece of paper—whether I'm young or old. I sold the first girl I loved, and she ran from me and my fat-fingered creditor both, and she threw herself off a high rock for all the world to see. She killed herself without another word between us. And you know what I done then? I come down out of these mountains and went off to the next town and gambled and sold some more until nothing could make me stop the selling. I even managed to sell you for a fair price, although we ain't got to that part yet. You might not recognize this child's face of mine, but you know the true shape of me. You know who I am."

And she did. Oh, she did, this gray-eyed Carolina boy. At some point, long before she met his adult body, he'd begun to call himself Hendricks—a name that now catapulted itself forward from her disassembled memory. He'd told her the story of his life, or as much of it as he could stand to tell before its misdeeds fully weighed him down. She had written out that life and memorized its every word. For him, she had left her imperiled home in an attempt to deliver the brittle gift of absolution. For the Hendricks she knew, she had even dabbled in the unbounded economy of what some would call love. And she'd been fooled. He had schemed her.

"So it's over and done with," she said, feeling a queer, watery flutter in her legs. She looked sorrowfully at the trumpet, which was now quite out of reach. "Your visit to me was never about the letter I could write for you. You lied to me, and I believed those lies. There's no one at the crossroads who needs to hear me speak the words in your letter. You don't even care if I get there. The girl you loved is dead. No one is waiting for you to confess a single deed. You've lured me out of my house, probably to destroy me."

"You kept your promise to me," the boy said, still pink and young in the cheeks. He seemed uneasy with her summary of things. He'd begun to pick at the knot on his trousers. "You been honorable. You tried to carry them words you wrote—and what they signify—from one place to the next. After all the walking we done together, and all the talking, I want to call it a fair swap even though you never got to fully finish your part in things. You been good to Mr. Hendricks, and good to me, too, every chance you had. But, yes ma'am, there was other trades on the offer sheet. There was other people, powerful ones, who wanted what they wanted. You had to be tricked out of your house. There was a wicked plot for it all. And now we're nearly done."

He took the red trumpet and placed it to his ageless lips.

"Stop," she whispered, suddenly aware that something had begun to stir within the ruined space of her belly, something wide-feeling and warm that coiled itself upward through the defeat that had been sluicing along her bones. It was a powerful force, this coiling. It heated her throat and pressed itself against the deep root of her tongue. "Stop a minute. There's one more thing I need to say, a piece I've remembered. I have some words for you. Please. These words. They go like this: *At this time in the valley of the river they call the Blackwater . . .*" And she closed her bleary eyes, hoping the boy would allow her to go on. Hoping against hope. The boy paused. He lowered the trumpet just an inch and looked squarely at her with his saltpeter eyes. This, she realized, was the true reason for her journey. The letter. Hendricks's letter was inside her. She had it with her, every word. And it was coming forth. She was telling it. This was what the council had wanted her to be prepared for. The letter knew Hendricks's future in ways his boy self did not. She had written it under the man's direction, and she could recite it now, detail after detail, and pray the boy would listen and glean and act to change his future. It was all a writer could do: lay out the consequences of a person's choices. Let him hear it all, she thought, her tongue furling with desperate eloquence. Let him listen to the story. Let him hear exactly who he is—and who he might yet become—before he decides which notes to blow.

Correspondence

Sister,

>Please forgive
>>the doll I stole
>>the kittens I starved
>>how mother loves me
>>how father loves me best
>>the dress I tore and its velvet buckles you liked so much
>>how I pretended you were invisible
>>how I wished you would disappear.

>Please forgive
>>the nights I wouldn't let you sleep
>>how I frightened you with stories.

Signature

She woke during the last hour of the day. What day? She didn't know. She didn't know how many nights had passed since she'd slithered from the belly of her house like a serpent driven forth by flood. Time had orphaned her. She had lost count of sun and moon. Everything had changed. The air she now breathed was thick with moisture and cool with the sympathies of twilight, and there was a careful wind whispering among the trees that leaned over her like attentive women of a certain age. The sky she could see was tasseled with reds and purples—the awning of a different, more credible world. She heard the clannish calls of geese, assembling one another in flight, rising. The questing whistle of a bobwhite yearned its way into her ears. She sensed houses too, or the remnants of houses. People had lived here once, and loved. Their desires still roamed the damp and sagging walls. For a brief moment, before her head cleared, she thought she heard the attenuated laughter of children dissipating with the daylight. The crossroads beneath the rock. She had gotten there. She had somehow made it to the place where all things intersected. Birds. Weather. The ambitions of men.

But he—the man she had traveled for—wasn't with her. And she was glad of it.

When she tested her legs, she found she didn't have the strength to stand. There was a needled feeling in the roof of her mouth, a flavor harsh and metallic, but she seemed to be herself again. Her body appeared to be her own—as emptied as it was. Even the familiar palsy in her left hand had returned. Physically, she was the woman she had always been before she met the man who called himself Hendricks. Except for the blood. There were pools of it beneath her, wet and warm.

She closed her eyes to rest them, and to slow the drumbeat of her pulse. This time, there was no dog to cajole or mystify her. And no boy to lead or mislead her. There were no followers gathered along a creek bank waiting for her next word. There was no final fragment of family, no shy petitioner hoping for a written letter, hat in hand. No one was waiting to construct a cairn in her memory—and that was how it should be. She didn't deserve to be remembered. She had substituted her own salvation for acts of honest courage. She had made a habit, an ugly habit, of trading unruly human love for payments she could hold tightly in her hands. She had discovered the flaw in that arrangement, the lonely annihilation of it, so late, too late, and now her time would end as it must. She would reap the thin harvest she had sowed.

She thought of the girl who had been Hendricks's first love, the one whose heart was so broken she had leaped from the highest rock she could find. Had the girl found peace as she took her wingless fall? Caring for the man called Hendricks was, it seemed, a cursed thing. She wondered how long it would take to complete her final plunge.

Not long, it seemed. They came quickly. And because they were not hiding themselves from anything or anyone, she could follow their approach. The orange fire of their torches flickered against the dark walls of their passage. She recognized the grinding roll of a two-wheeled cart, a large one. She wondered if they were rovers, members of the straggling bands that foraged the mountains to their own advantage. Rovers would strip her naked before she died. If they were Billy's men, the ones with harnesses and hounds, her fate would be even worse.

The cart was drawn by some kind of pony, a plodding cross-breed imported with the hope it would survive a while. She had never seen one like it, sleek, with a coat the color of ripe peaches stirred with cream. Torchlight splashed across its rump like spilling water. It seemed to sigh with every step it took, as if its burden was constantly increasing. She didn't recognize the pony, but she knew the men in the cart it pulled all too well. Death would have been far more welcome.

Billy Kingery sat upright at the reins wearing a topcoat as smooth and black as his hair. Hendricks was behind him in the rickety bed of the cart. Her Hendricks. The full-grown man who had plagued both her dreams and her designs. He was clad in the same patched jacket he had worn during their few days together at her house. The same smoke-tinted shirt. His body was slumped against the cart's makeshift rails, his face swollen with drunkenness and misery. He was surrounded by several large sacks tied off with rope and string.

"Your two days is up and then some," Billy said. He spoke loudly as if she lay a great distance from him. "It took me a good part of that time to get this far given my slow conveyance. I'm proud to say you was even slower."

She couldn't speak and didn't want to. Everything observant within her had shrunk to a single burning pinpoint near her heart. Hendricks was riding with Billy Kingery? As if it hadn't been enough to be swindled by him in boy form during the journey that was dream and not-dream, she had to see him now, when she was wrecked and dying? Not long before she had wanted to meet him at the crossroads. She had wanted it very much. But not with Billy. That wasn't part of the arrangement. And he wasn't trussed up as Billy's prisoner either. Which could mean only one thing.

"Come on, talk to us, girl. We know you got things to say." Billy halted the cart close to her feet. The pony, whose forelock covered its pony eyes, lowered its head in profound relief. "Two days passage," Billy chortled. "I asked you not to touch my property or injure my men. You done both when you consorted with Hendricks here. You broke every rule I gave."

She wanted Hendricks to look at her. She seemed to be propped against some sort of stone wall, stashed there like an abandoned bedroll. The torches lashed to the corners of the cart cast a blue, obscuring smoke. And the light of day continued to fade. Yet she needed Hendricks to see her—to acknowledge her—no matter what he'd done or not done, no matter what he knew or didn't know about Billy Kingery and the ghost boy version of himself who had led her here. She wouldn't allow him to pretend she didn't matter. She tried to draw herself into a sturdier posture, but failed. Her spine wasn't working right. And there was a dangerous, thudding ache between her legs.

"Don't say you didn't hurt nobody," Billy continued, filling in her side of the conversation since she wasn't playing her part. "Because you did. You brung on injury when this one took a arrow in your defense." He gestured a gloved hand at Hendricks. "He's been in my pocket more than a year, ever since he failed to pay the debt he owed on his most recent wife. He is *mine*. I tried to tell you how unreliable he was when you come ministrating into my store. I mentioned the wife he sold. She's one of several he's had—not that you was counting. But you didn't take the hint. You thought you was on a mission that mattered. The fact is, *nothing* matters unless I say it does. I'm the one who makes the plans. You've damaged my property. You broke my rules. Ask him yourself."

She raised her head again to Hendricks. He sagged like a man who was terminally inebriated. Soused with it. "I owed," he said, not lifting his eyes. "It weren't no more than that."

The worst of it was how she would now have to cross the final span utterly alone. She wasn't afraid of dying, or fighting to her death if she could find some way to do it. She would love to cost Billy Kingery a pound of flesh before she left this world. But, despite her self-imposed solitude, she had always hoped there would be someone—a tender member of the Uninvited, a substitute sister, maybe even a wandering fellow like Hendricks—willing to take note of her final hour. "Is the house all right?" she asked, trying to keep her voice dignified and smooth.

"The house is *mine*," Billy said. "Just like I been planning. I told Alton Altice he can have it, but that arrangement won't last any longer than Alton does. His end will come soon. Then I can put somebody in there who will run things right. Or maybe I'll let those scallywag boys of Alton's piss all through the place, then light the match."

"It won't burn," she said, coughing. The searing taste in her mouth had become stronger. It was as if there were coals glowing somewhere near the roots of her teeth, and Billy's words were howling right across those coals. She wished she had a knife to throw. Or a sharp stone.

"It'll burn if I say it needs to burn," Billy said. "Same with that camp of vagrants or whatever you call them. There'll be real fine entertainment in that field when the time comes to clean them out. A regular military display."

"You said you'd give . . . you're giving them people to me," Hendricks blurted, stirring himself amid the crowd of sacks. "You said I'd get my pick. I need sales. They got children in that camp. Children bring a good price. I got more debts to pay."

Billy eyeballed his woeful companion. "I said a lot of things. Some is truer than others. We'll get you sorted when the time comes, don't you worry."

"But you promised—"

Billy slapped Hendricks so quickly she didn't even see it. She could hear it, however, the crack of a gloved hand across an unready face. She heard it several times.

"I promised you'd be free when we was done. That's all. Free and clear. Anything else you claim is part of some tale you been telling inside your pitiful drunkard's head. Did you ever explain to this woman what put you in prison the first time? With all that sweet lover's time to talk, all that confessing and manliness you acted out in front of her so you could get her to trust you—did you ever tell her how you got your start?"

She saw Hendricks paw at his face. The letter she'd written for him had accounted for many crimes. But he hadn't spoken of his time in prison. There were parts of himself he hadn't shared, not even with her. She had been bewitched by him, nonetheless. Worse yet, she had failed to peg him as a servant—a spy—of Billy Kingery. As bad as he was, she hadn't believed he was capable of that.

"I want you to know why this is happening," Billy said, facing her again. "I want you to appreciate my plan. It's a fact I covet your house and land. And I'll take revenge on your dead sister any way I can. She cost me a wife and two boy babies, the most pitiful innocents I ever seen. But this is mostly about how things have got to go in this country, to make things work right again. Gathering and organizing. Barter and trade. This is about showing people how they got to live—together."

"It was debt," Hendricks mumbled from between his swelling lips. He was without his hat, his head looking more narrow and carved-on than ever. She saw that Billy allowed him to keep a jug close at hand. It seemed to be his only ally. "I owed."

"We all owe," she said.

"Some more than others," Billy said, laughing out of one side of his white-toothed mouth. "You was harder to pry out of that house than your sister was, I'll give you that. But I found my bait when I needed it. A letter. You gave it all away for this man's goddamned *letter*."

Hendricks stopped his swaying, if only for an instant. He was a wretch and as good a liar as she'd ever met, but he wasn't immune to mockery. She could see that.

"Maybe it was worth it," she said.

"Ain't nothing worth bleeding in the road like a butchered hog," Billy said, peering down at her. "Look at you. I've seen saggy-tit sows die with less mess. You don't got much time left."

She planted her hands on either side of her body and propped herself up as straight as she could manage. "Then it's good . . . it's a good thing I finished what I started," she said. "The letter was delivered."

Billy scratched at his shiny head with a glove. "Hush up. You ain't had time to deliver nothing but your own self right here. The girl he loved killed herself. Her bones is with the worms. You got nobody to give a letter *to*. A paper like that ain't got no power, anyhow. I've took everything you own. That's the only score I'm keeping."

She let him talk. Men who were used to getting what they wanted yammered. They believed people needed to hear all the words they chose to say. The colonel at Fishersville had been a yammerer. And it had finally cost him. A flat-chested ten-year-old had stabbed him in the black hole of his ear with a needle while he was delivering one of his bare-assed monologues. Billy Kingery could speechify all he wanted, but Hendricks, perched on the cart, was listening only to her. She knew it.

"I can't . . . I won't share the details of another man's deal." She tried not to cough between her words. "It's not allowed. But the letter was memorized and . . . and delivered. Ask him. He knows it. He believes me."

"Frog shit," Billy said. "I ought to get down from here and shovel you into your grave right now."

"Please do," she said, closing her eyes again. "I'd consider it a favor."

"What are you saying?" Hendricks asked, half-standing in the cart.

"I think I understand it now." She tried, once more, to pull herself upright. Once more, she failed. The blood beneath her had spread as wide as a bridal skirt. "I was supposed to . . . to hurry to this place. But you knew I wouldn't find anybody, even if . . . if I got here."

"Her family's been gone a long time. Mine, too," Hendricks said, his voice fading.

"I might be getting tired of this," Billy said, pantomiming a yawn. "I might be ready to end this and get back home."

"There ain't . . . none of them left," Hendricks said, lowering himself and his jug to the floor of the cart. His eyes looked like bore holes in his head. "I'm the last one on this earth."

"I met a boy on the road," she said. "I think you'd know him."

"That trumpet boy is dead," Billy said, impatient. "My man Hendricks here killed him in a blink. No mercy. No thinking. Which is how it has to be."

"Lots of boys are dead," she said as loudly as she could. "But not this one. You . . . you know who I'm talking about, Hendricks. Tell him. Tell Billy Kingery who heard me recite your letter."

"I never told her about us," Hendricks said to Billy, standing again. The cart jolted under his movement. The sacks inside seemed to lean toward him, jostling him with their weight and contents, but the pony, as weary as it was, held fast. "I never told her nothing about our deal. She didn't suspect a thing. I swear."

"It don't matter," Billy said, rolling his eyes. "Get down off there and end this. It's getting late."

"It *does* matter," Hendricks shouted. "You make like you're the collector of all the debts in the world, but I didn't trade you this one. I got to settle with her. It's my right."

"Hell and high water, I am up to my neck in sanctity and indignation." Billy sighed. "I'll say it one more time, man. Get down off there and slit her throat. You won't like the price I'll charge if I have to do it myself. Not one bit."

She spoke softly, for that's all she had the strength to do. "I met him," she said. "I traveled with the boy you used to be. He's a kind child at the bottom of his heart. He took care of me."

Hendricks appeared confused, barely able to maintain his balance in the back of the cart. "I . . . I don't know what—"

"Come . . . come down here," she said. "Come down where we can talk."

And he did. He vaulted over the side of the cart with the quick strength she remembered. He landed hard on both feet, wincing because of his wounded leg, but close enough that she knew she would smell him soon, his warm musk, and all of his betrayals.

"You'll need my knife, " Billy said.

"I won't need a damn thing," he replied. He squatted next to her, the toes of his boots not quite touching the dark hem of her blood. "Does it hurt?"

"Not anymore. The cold is coming. It's . . . it's up past my knees. Can I say it's good to see you?"

"No," he said. "Don't lie to me."

"It's not a lie. You . . . you've sold everything you ever loved. I know that. You've sold me too. But you gave me . . . the chance to do what I was meant to do. That boy—the one who's like some untouched part of you—he listened to what we wrote together. He learned the story of who he would become. I . . . I don't know what that means, exactly. I can't see the end of it. I don't know if the boy can change himself, if you can be changed. Maybe it was a waste of time. Or . . . or maybe what he heard will make a difference in what you do or say, how you settle things with Billy. I . . . don't know what will happen. Tell me. Please. In . . . in the past two days did you ever hear my voice?"

"I ain't nothing but a criminal." She saw that he'd begun to weep. She tried to raise her hand to him, up toward his dampened face, but couldn't. "A criminal made worse by every crime. That man up yonder, and others like him, has showed me paths more scathing than death, and I've took them every time. I come to your house under false pretense, with the worst intentions of all. I come to help him take all that you had. And you treated me decent. You . . . you . . ." He couldn't go on. "When Billy gives that knife, you should gut me with it."

Above them, Billy Kingery gave two impatient cracks with his whip. The pony was almost too tired to respond, but it tried. The cart rolled forward half a turn. The torches tilted and spewed. The sacks inside the cart contracted and curled as if they were alive. "There ain't a scheme in this world that'll save her," he said, wearily. "You'd best quit your whispering. My man Blankenship will be here soon. Conklin and Cundiff are with him. They got a whole passel of stalking dogs out looking for this woman. I'd hate to ask them to wade into this situation when all I'm trying to do is spare some suffering. It's meant to be painless, Hendricks. A clean cut below the ears."

"I know how to slit a throat," Hendricks said.

"I reckon you do." Billy slipped off one of his tight and shining gloves. "You'll need this."

Before he stood to take the knife, Hendricks dropped a small disk from his sleeve, a tiny, glittering lens. It fell close to the trembling curl of her left hand. As she reached to touch it, he brushed her face briefly with his fingers, in perfect memory of a moth's gentle wings. There was almost a smile on his face as he did so, a final slanting shard.

"From your daddy's scope," he murmured. "I watched the stars all night after you left me. I seen wonders and beauties and never forgot you for a minute, I swear. Things is not what they seem. Your letter made it through to me. Do you hear? *There is no fortress for the man who puts himself above the sanctity of others.* Do you hear me? The letter got through. I have brung help. Things is *not* what they seem right now."

And he stood to face Billy.

They would later tell many versions of his escape, the man who came to the brick house above the creek for a letter or some kind of queer service and was drawn into fighting with the large brood of Altices who lived nearby and then fell to battling the migrant people, wanted or unwanted, who camped in those fields and maintained a worship of the healing they believed came from the brick house and the strange sisters who lived there. They told all manner of tale about how he got away, none of them verified, each bloodier than the last. They blamed him for the fire that burned to cinder all but the stone-lined kitchen of the sisters' house. They blamed him for the drought that dried up their springs and wells, as if the trespasses he committed had the power to redirect water. They blamed him for the violent feuding that led to the murder of Alton Altice by his brother Willem. They blamed him for the poor corn crop and the ice that remained thick on their ponds until March and the unseasonal attacks of owls. They blamed him for the disrespect of their children, each and every antagonism they had to endure from the sons and daughters who were inspired by the exploits of young Bofrane Altice and his fearless cousin Tul. They blamed him for every habit they couldn't change, and for the ones they chose not to, and they didn't stop talking about him, liquor in hand, pipes lit and burning, wives and husbands hitched against their hips, for more years than any of them could count.

It's said he didn't use the tunnel that ran from the cellar of the house. He chose, instead, that silvery moment on the cusp of night when even the finest hunters question the ghostly, untethered movements of their prey. He slipped away like a gust of wind. The Altices were drunk, every last son and bitch of them. They maintained themselves that way. The Uninvited were the ones he watched for. They would skewer a man bloodless.

Yet he was no stealthier than the two boys. They were waiting for him beneath the cascading tresses of a willow tree—one tall, the other not. As if he were a comet destined to flare across their sky.

"We knowed you'd come," Bofrane said, leaning against a sharpened gig that was nearly as long as he was. "Tul had the sense of it. He's got the gift."

"Let me pass."

"This ain't about stopping you," Bofrane said. "This is about crossing the river and finding that woman, which is something me and Tul can do better than you. We know the country."

The smaller boy tilted his head, mouth a half-stitched seam. His hair was braided with duckweed and mud.

"You gonna turn me over to your daddy?"

"We hate my daddy. Uncle Willem's the one we aim to join with. You and your pistol can help us. And we like the woman. It ain't no more than that."

They agreed to travel together. The man Hendricks knew the cousins might be useful, especially given his wounded leg.

They crossed the river at a place that did not require swimming. The waters bowed toward them beneath the black cowl of night, cold and deep and quiet, the current so smooth it didn't even hiss. Bofrane claimed any man who entered the river with a true heart would be carried safely across. "I ain't much for water," he said. "Tul likes to sass me for it." Young Tul, for his part, slipped from the bank as smoothly as a mink.

As the water grappled the man known as Hendricks in its icy, uncaring arms, he thought of the woman. The journey he had conspired to send her on was a perilous one. He didn't believe she was dead, not yet. But she was in danger—danger he had practically forged with his own hands. He hoped she had laid claim to some of her sister's power. Memory of the alluring voice that had come from the woman's unwilling mouth hitched knots in the flow of his mercenary blood. The sister was like no conjurer he'd ever encountered. Nevertheless, he had successfully lured the woman from her home as ordered by Billy Kingery. Now he was pursuing her, against orders, against the tide of Billy's plans. Things had gone topsy-turvy. He had been transformed. Because the woman had become something to him, something he dared not name. As he recalled her face, he was reminded of a portrait he'd once stolen from the wall of a great house, the brooding eyes that could not be dissuaded by riot or greed. He clamored to see eyes like those again.

The boys trotted confidently through the tangled brush on the other side of the river. "This is the easy part," Bofrane said, wiping his snotty child's nose. "Ain't nobody organized over here. Billy don't allow it."

Silent Tul made as if to spit between Hendricks's sopping boots as they paused. It was his way of asking if Hendricks knew who Billy Kingery was.

"I know him. I've wore his chains. But I ain't wearing them now."

Tul assessed him, shirtsleeves dripping. Then he nudged his cousin with an elbow.

"Tul needs to know you got good intentions toward that woman," Bofrane said.

"I aim to show my good intentions—and more—when I find her. I aim to tell her the truth about how she's changed me. The rest will be what it'll be."

This time, Tul spit for real.

"I ain't asking you to believe me yet," he said to the boy. "I got plenty to prove. But not everything a man does with other men is pegged to trust. Some nights you hunt with the pack you find."

When Tul stopped at a creek that was tiled with smooth stone, Bofrane declared it was time for them to rest. The younger cousin climbed a nearby tree without a word.

"He'll hang up there like a bat," Bofrane said. "Watching. We can get our sleep."

He opened his eyes some hours later to find Bofrane standing over him, breath stenchy with wild onion. "It's time," the boy declared. "I hope you ain't hungry cause we don't have nothing we want to share."

"How far?"

"You ain't seen how Tul makes a path, have you? He does it with a piece of mirror he keeps around his neck. He stares at the damn thing and marks it with his fingers until he's ready. He ain't never done us wrong."

They skirted homesteads and the remnants of farms. They smelled the sheep-stink of boiled blankets and heard the clucking of hungry hens, but Tul knew who had dogs and burros, and who did not, so they passed unmolested. After a long passage of silence, Bofrane asked Hendricks if he believed what the woman did with the writing of letters was a real power.

Hendricks said he did.

"My daddy says her sister could raise the dead. He hates them both. I'd like to have the power of taming animals myself. I'd tame a bear or a eagle, or maybe a ocean whale. You ever hear about the girl from the Knott's Island who coughs up pearls? They say she was born that way. I don't know how a thing like that happens, but I do like a pearl."

"Riches ain't always what they seem," Hendricks said.

"Maybe not. I could tell you a story on that score if you wanted. It's one our granny tells, a hunting story that features cousins such as Tul and me."

And so he began to tell it, as if he couldn't help himself. How a batch of cousins took their batch of good dogs and went way up into the hills to hunt coons. They went to a place they'd never been before, and they turned the dogs loose, and the dogs caught a scent and set to running and baying their tunes. They ran like nobody had ever heard them run before, crazed with the idea of catching whatever they were after. And caught it they did. Caught it and killed it and mangled it until it wasn't recognizable as a coon or anything else.

"A stunt like that gets dogs shot," Bofrane said. "But nobody shot a dog that night. They set up camp and waited to see if the dogs would run again."

But the dogs didn't run. They seemed barely inclined to try. When the cousins got hungry, one of them decided to take the tender bits that remained from the creature the dogs had killed and roast them over the fire. They ate and drank more whiskey, until one of the meaner cousins decided to get even with the dogs. When one of them slunk close to the fire, he threw it into the flames.

Cussing and wrestling transpired because the mean cousin was not loved by any of them, but a dog had value. They only stopped their wrestling when they saw the dog at the bottom of the cliff looking as good as new.

"You can guess what happened next," Bofrane said. "That mean cousin bellered out a claim or two, then walked hisself right into the fire."

"And lived to tell about it?"

"He ended up at the bottom of the cliff too. The rest of them was so amazed, they—"

The boy stopped. They both heard it. The sound of something scampering through the woods, fast.

"I hope it's Tul," Bofrane whispered. "'Cause there ain't no caution to its passage."

It was Tul, looking devious and triumphant. He waved his prize proudly, an ear of corn still steaming in its husk.

"Oh, hell," Bofrane said. "I should've knowed he was up to something. The boy's got a weakness for roasted corn."

"He been robbing a washerwoman?" Hendricks asked.

"Tul ain't attracted to easy crime," Bofrane said. "I expect there's more than one of them. But Tul's in the mood for a raid."

"We have a choice?"

"Not really," Bofrane replied. "I've tried walking off when he wants something. It don't turn out so good."

The men were camped at a tumbledown sawmill. There were three of them lounging around a slow-burning fire. They had a pack of hounds with them, lean, sweat-crusted wraiths they'd locked in a shed. Hendricks knew who they had to be: a trio of Billy Kingery's acquisitive bargain men. They were hunting something or someone.

"This ain't a good idea," Hendricks said to Bofrane.

"It ain't."

"Why so reckless?"

"Tul's hungry. And it's in our blood. Nobody ever pinned a medal on a Altice for being smart."

It's said the plan was for Tul to steal the corn while the men were looking another way. He would create a distraction. And sure enough, the high-pitched screams of what sounded like a dying rabbit soon rang out from the edge of the clearing, drawing the attention of the men and their hounds. The men were tempted by the prospect of roasting rabbit with their corn, especially if they could steal it from the hawk or fox that had gotten to it first.

Rabbit-voiced Tul appeared next to the fire quick as a snap. All he had to do was scoop up the corn and be gone. But one of the men ambled around a whipsaw platform when he was least expected. He sent up the alarm straightaway.

It's said Bofrane Altice revealed his hiding place out of desperation. He aimed to save his cousin. Tul had been collared by the bargain man. He was wriggling like a mudpuppy in a gill net when Hendricks also stepped into the clearing and fired his pistol. The bargain man went down, gut shot. Tul rolled clear, and Hendricks was looking for a way he and the boys could beat a retreat when he heard a sound behind him. Turning, he saw Bofrane impaled on his own sharpened gig, the victim of a second bargain man. The older cousin had flung himself into the path of the ambusher, a snake-eyed fellow as thin as fence wire, only to find himself skewered with his own weapon. Bofrane had covered Hendricks's back, and it had cost him.

Hendricks flushed the snake-eyed bargain man from his position behind a tree and shot him dead. He grabbed the man's hanks of hair and cut his throat for good measure.

There was also the third bargain man. Hendricks dared not tend to Bofrane until he was accounted for. He needn't have worried. Tul was waiting when the third man hauled himself back into the clearing. With one stroke, Tul split the man's skull with his wicked little hatchet. Then he returned to the first fellow, who was rooting like a pig in the dirt, blind with agony from the wound in his gut. The smaller cousin measured the man's neck for a final blow. Behind him, the skeletal hounds flung themselves at the walls of the shed and bayed with futility into the afternoon.

It's said Hendricks tore at his own shirt to make some kind of bandage, but Bofrane, rigid with pain, shook his head, and Tul, lungs heaving from the ordeal of it all, shook his head also. There was nothing to be done for Bofrane. Except a swift act of mercy.

The man Hendricks was distraught. They had risked everything for damned roasted corn. They had exposed themselves, and made a mortal enemy of Billy Kingery, and gotten Bofrane killed all at once. "You know who they was?" he shouted. "You know who'll be coming for us now?" But his anger didn't distract Tul Boitnott, nor move him one inch from his cousin's side.

Hendricks tried to steady himself. "You expect me to do it, you impulsive pup? All right then. I'll end your cousin's pain because he protected me when he weren't sworn to do so. But I won't have nothing more to do with you. You'll get to your uncle on your own."

It's said the man Hendricks then swallowed a whole string of sobs as he bent over Bofrane Altice. The boy gave permission. By the time the knife blade was placed at an angle beneath the beardless chin, the light in those amiable blue eyes was nearly gone.

In the end, Hendricks wasn't able to rid himself of Tul Boitnott. The boy helped loot the sawmill for weapons and supplies, although he didn't touch the corn. He found a resting place for Bofrane in the fork of an alder tree that allowed for honorable views of sky and valley alike, and he released the confused hounds from the shed. He also declined to leave Hendricks's side, even when he was cuffed and kicked. He didn't have to speak. His intentions were clear. Bargain men had killed Bofrane Altice. Bargain men worked for Billy Kingery. It was time to get even with Billy Kingery.

"You got any idea what we're in for?" Hendricks asked. "I'm following that woman. I bet you every string on your mandolin them men was doing the same. Billy didn't get where he's at by making hisself vulnerable. He counts on others to make the mistakes. I'll have to lie and sneak and playact right up to the edge of destruc-

tion to get close to him again. I'll have to convince him he's master.
I can't go into a fight like that with a boy—a child—who makes
fool choices like the one you just made."

Tul observed him as if he were an empty anthill. Or a paw print
pressed into dry soil. Then he faced the alder where Bofrane rested,
and he looked at it for a long while, fingering the pouch he wore
strapped around his neck, the one that contained the bit of mirror
he used to select his paths.

"What's it gonna be?" asked soldier Hendricks. "Can you be a
man of caution? Or are you destined to act the fool?"

It's said Tul Boitnott slipped his chunk of mirror from its pouch.
He fixed his eyes upon his trusted coin of glass as if it were the
deepest of deep mountain lakes. He stared into the mirror before
he raised it to Hendricks's face and bade him look at the smeared
and shrunken portrait of himself reflected there. This was Tul
Boitnott's response, a question of his own: Was fickle Hendricks
prepared to assess the mask of his brutality? Could he, once and
for all, be true?

He could.

So Tul Boitnott squeezed the mirror tight between his small,
capable hands until it caught no light at all. Then he looked at his
partner Hendricks, and spit.

Billy Kingery was done with delays. Irritated by Hendricks's moony
talk with the woman who lay bleeding beside the road, he raised
his whip once more. He would lash Hendricks. Harshly. As many
times as it took. But he was interrupted by what sounded like a
loud trumpet call. The brassy, wavering notes seemed to come from
all around him—from the right and the left, from the east and the
west, from above and below. Then, as quickly as it had started, the
trumpet stopped.

"That's my men," Billy said, standing high and confident in the seat of the pony cart, the whip gripped tightly in his hands. "About damn time they got here."

"It ain't your men," Hendricks said. He was off-kilter himself. The trumpet call surprised him. He had been planning what he imagined would be a flagrant duel between himself and Billy, a reckoning staged with weapons fair and unfair where he, given his many pirate skills, might have a small chance to prevail. He felt ready, and strengthened, because the woman had learned the truth of him. He was on her side and would remain there. If he died, he died unburdened. He also knew sly Tul Boitnott was waiting in the woods in case he failed with Billy. But their plan did not involve a signal from a trumpet.

"Blankenship is coming," Billy declared. "With Cundiff and Conklin and the dogs. I set it up."

"The bugle call ain't from them," Hendricks said, smiling grimly. "They been delayed."

"Not possible." Billy readied his whip again. "Blankenship follows my orders. You don't know—"

"If Blankenship's the skinny one with the viper eyes, I *do* know. I killed him myself. All three of them is dead and gone. I spared the dogs."

Billy tried to pretend he wasn't shocked by the news. He began an immediate assault upon Hendricks, lifting his whip high into the air and unleashing it toward the man's unprotected face. But the whip had acquired a mind of its own. It curled and laced and luffed more like silk ribbon than braided leather as it made its way downward. Its lash finally rested upon Hendricks's shoulder as softly as a mother's caress.

"Well, I'll be double damned," Billy cursed, staring at the recalcitrant whip as though it had stung him. "This is nonsense. I got to get serious." He dropped the whip and reached to unbutton his long black coat. As he did so, the invisible trumpet sounded once more.

It was this second chorus that roused her from her stupor. She knew that horn. She knew those notes—although they sounded more glorious to her now than ever before. Estefan, her Estefan. His summoning tones seemed to resonate everywhere, spreading outward from where she lay until the very rim of twilight became pure, harmonious quiver. There was a sense of profound, continuing disturbance within and around her. She felt it hum through her defeated body. It was something like a sea wind, but not. Like a thousand million insects vibrating in the hot summer trees, but not. Like the quiet, castaway murmurs of the dead, but not quite.

She was able to pull herself to her feet with a new strength, and she suddenly understood what she must do. For not only had Billy Kingery's whip become useless to him, he was now in the process of discovering he was no longer able to unfasten the large black buttons on his coat. The buttons would not let themselves be undone. So he could not get to his other weapons save the small knife he'd offered to Hendricks and that knife had somehow become glued to the black glove on Billy's hand. Billy's feet had become tightly fused to the floorboards of the pony cart as well, and she could see exactly what needed to happen next. It was perfect. A parade. The occasion called for a parade. And she knew just how the procession should go. The pony, also instilled with fresh vigor, seemed more than ready to serve as her companion. It began to step forward as soon as she reached its side.

Above her, Billy Kingery stopped tearing at his coat buttons just long enough to offer a prince-like entreaty. "Hendricks," he hollered. "Come here, man. We ain't settled our business yet. I'll pay whatever you ask. We can forget about Blankenship and them. We can call it square. I just need you to come to *me*."

She could not see Hendricks or anything beyond Billy and the rolling cart. The pony had somehow found the energy to jog, squaring its pony shoulders as though it was being coaxed along by additional handlers who were invisible to her. She felt the infusion of a new communion within her blood and heart. She was no longer alone. Our parade, she told herself. It was time to create for Billy Kingery his own kind of ceremony. It didn't matter that she couldn't see the other participants. She knew they were there. She could sense them all around her, a happy throng, its many feet moving in shared rhythm, its joyous momentum echoed by the unseen rollicking of goats and dogs. A parade. One she had finally been invited to join.

Billy Kingery, however, was not about to suffer his voyage in silence.

"You don't know what you're doing," he shouted at Hendricks and at her, leaning from one side of the cart to the other as if he were trying to see who or what, besides the two of them, had taken control of the situation. "You ain't obeying the rules. I don't know who you're working for, or who's put you up to this, but you can't make private pandemonium like this. It ain't allowed. My men are coming. They will take you down—all of you. You can't ignore the rules."

Yet the more he beseeched, the more nimbly the pony advanced and the more the great sacks stored in the bed of the cart began to shift toward him, their ropes and strings loosening and falling away as though they were being untied by invisible hands. Whatever was in those sacks seemed to be escaping from them. Freely.

Hendricks stood rooted in place, frozen with confusion and awe. He and the boy Tul had traveled hard and fast. They had caught sight of Billy and his loaded cart in time for Hendricks to slink his way into Billy's good graces. But it seemed that neither Billy's fate nor Tul's was his to influence. He could only watch as the pony trotted onward with the woman's pale hand gripping its harness, its pony head lifted as if to mimic a general's fearsome stallion. High in a defiant elm tree that bowered across the neglected road, Hendricks saw a winking flash, a miniature star of light like that which might be produced by a small fragment of mirror. He knew that light, oh he did. It meant Tul Boitnott was up in that elm—waiting for his chance. All Hendricks could do was watch as the truculent shape of a hand-fashioned noose appeared below the branches of the tree. Which meant the speechless cousin of the late Bofrane Altice was ready to take his revenge, no hatchet needed. Which meant there would be no escape for Billy Kingery.

"You can't do this," Billy screeched, gloved hands gripping and tearing at his polished hair. "I rule it all. I'm the rule."

The trumpet sounded for a third time, more forlorn but no less convincing. Its final notes seemed to resound from earth to sky, wrapping even the great pinnacle of stone that rose above them in its tune. The clarion call drove the woman to her knees. She fell away from the insistent, trotting pony. The cart and its unspeakable baggage rolled forward without her, all the way to the end of its inexplicable route. Hendricks saw the cart bounce into the knuckled shadows of the elm until it was directly beneath the noose. He saw the dandling shape of the rope blend with the waggling shape of Billy's head. He listened as Billy's final curses were transformed into an unholy thrashing until he could listen no more. Tul Boitnott did not fail.

Then, for him, the one who had long ago adopted the name Hendricks when he required the convenience of a new start, there remained only the woman. Billy Kingery had been taken beyond them. All that separated the two of them now were their private wounds and reluctances. They could still hope for redemption, could they not? He ran to her even as a kind of wintry fog began to granulate the air around them. He could not locate its source as he ran. It seemed to rise from the trampled crust of the ground, and it bore within its gathering whiteness the promise of a tender, early snow. He felt its insistent cold in contrast to the fiery pounding of his heart. He had arrived at the crossroads too late—too late—and he despised himself for it.

The woman, lying in the muddy, wheel-scored path made by the pony cart, did not seem to notice him when he reached her. She appeared to be talking to someone else, settling something with words so soft he could not hear them at all. He could see she was nearly gone, her blanched hands lying flat across her sunken chest, her breath as shallow as a sparrow's. Yet there was a bewildered contentment in the curve of her cheeks he had never seen before. He bent and lifted her from the cradle of her own fresh blood.

"Who's talking?" he asked. "You need to save your strength."

"You know her," she whispered. "You've talked to her. We are making our peace, just the two of us. I don't need anything else, not even my strength. She says you still owe us a haul of wood, though. We expect our pay." And she tried to laugh.

"You will get the last . . . the last honest toil of me that's ever offered in this world," he said. And he kissed the face he had wanted so badly to see again, the lips and nose and brow that were already too white and too cold.

"It's all right," she said, her head nestling against the strong bough of his neck.

"It ain't," he said, swallowing the freshet of his tears. "We worked ourselves to a new place, new to both of us. And you give up everything for me. But I got here slow. I was too slow."

"No. Hush. You led me to her again, my sister. And you led me into your own self. You came when I was ready."

He lifted her higher in his arms in response, wrapping her more tightly as he sensed new, strange currents all around them, flowing and grasping currents he felt the urge to flee. He wanted her for himself. They deserved their time together, surely they did. Just a day, or an hour. He tried to frame a plea with his mouth even as he recognized the rime of frost that had begun to form on his boots, and hers.

"There's one more thing I need to find," she said. "Will you take me to it?"

He gazed into her eyes, those confounding portrait eyes, and he understood, although the understanding pierced him through and through. She knew what she wanted at the last. It was not what he had hoped for. All he had hoped for was a chance. Just one. And he would not get it. As the first skirl of snow began to veil them in its merciless lace, he felt the shifting ballast of her departure even as she drew herself closer within his embrace. Memory of that frail and dwindling weight would never leave him. He would carry it the rest of his life. He said to her, "I will."

"I nearly missed you, you know," she said, pausing briefly to taste the blood that had finally made its way to her tongue. "I wasn't ready to give anything to you . . . or to anybody. But I've sampled what might have been, and I'm being welcomed by those who care for me. I haven't been forgotten, or judged. I'm not being left behind, and . . . and that matters more than you can know. You can still make a family for yourself. It's not too late. You can give what love and trust you have to those who need it—even if it's not to me. Will you make that promise?"

He didn't know how to answer. Some years later he would be presented with the opportunity to protect a red-haired woman and her bastard son, and he would seize that opportunity as if it were a golden treasure and he would not let it go. He attributed those days of fragile, but honest, happiness to the woman he met at the brick house above the creek, the one who had reluctantly, and ferociously, written the letter of his life.

Yet even though he would dream of her each time the moon waxed fat and full, there was much about that final hour at the crossroads he would never understand. He was never entirely sure who or what had rescued the two of them from the brute ending they had likely faced at the hands of Billy Kingery, although in truth, there was no rescue—the woman he had come to love would die that day. His own life would end later, on a contentious and absurd afternoon not yet notched in the belt of the minion who would finally draw his straw. But they had not been parted without a final embrace, or a chance to revise the telling as they wished. It's said the love between them became a force all its own in those final moments, that the great rock at the crossroads split top to bottom from that force, and the wound in the rock became a sign to all who passed of what was true in the world and what was false. She was taken from him, nonetheless.

And with the taking came another pilgrimage, this one more solemn than the first but also with its joys and resolutions. As he bore her in his arms, he heard what seemed to be the patter of children's feet all around them. Also the sure, wayfaring steps of mothers and fathers. The contented swishing of skirts and shoes and scarves. And the murmurs of many languages. Could it be the sister's doing, all of it, even the haunting solos of a single beloved trumpet? He didn't know. He knew only that he was carrying the woman as she had asked him to, that he was walking into the beseeching shadows cast by an ageless spire of stone, sensing with each step that they were being joined by others, that his strength was being shared and multiplied.

He was momentarily afraid he would see faces alongside them that he knew, the faces of his dead and mistreated, but he did not. This was the woman's reckoning, not his, and the scores being settled were hers alone. He felt her last breaths warm against the bare hollow of his throat. He felt her bones settle without wariness against his own. But as the sun he thought he knew extinguished itself against the old breast of the old mountains, she was taken from him, borne aloft into a weightlessness he could not fathom or follow. He was left behind as she was lifted, although not by water; as she was set free, although not in body. The silence that finally buoyed her was kinder than any silence he had ever known.

Acknowledgments

Connor Southard, Melchora Alexander, and Mandy Hoy were early readers and aided me immensely with their questions and insights. Gail Hochman read brilliantly as she always does and helped me untangle some tight knots. Jim Southard, Sharon Southard, John Mittelstaedt, and Patrice Noel gave me access to their lovely, quiet homes so I could write. Meade and Andrea Dominick provided time on the gorgeous 7D Ranch. Harold Bergman hosted me at the historic AMK Ranch. Beth Kephart kept the faith. The University of Wyoming granted me a delicious sabbatical. Bob Southard provided much necessary laughter, patience, and time on good rivers.

The team at Graywolf Press is truly without parallel. It is impossible to express enough gratitude for their expertise, energy, and excellence. Fiona McCrae, Marisa Atkinson, Casey O'Neil, Susannah Sharpless, and Caroline Nitz all played critical roles in the completion of this book. As for Katie Dublinski, what can I say? This is our fifth project together, and I am beyond blessed.

I thought of my aunt Lois Lindsay Brown many times while I was writing this book. I wondered what she would think of it and my irreverent pilfering of various sources and myths. Elements of the Jack Tales appear here, as do family legends, borrowed character names, regional histories, and narratives rooted in indigenous cultures. Lois was the keeper of our family tales. She is no longer with us, but I like to think she's still collecting good stories somewhere.

Alyson Hagy was raised on a farm in the Blue Ridge Mountains of Virginia. She is the author of seven previous works of fiction, most recently *Boleto*. She lives in Laramie, Wyoming.

The text of *Scribe* is set in Adobe Garamond Pro. Book design by Rachel Holscher. Composition by Bookmobile Design and Digital Publisher Services, Minneapolis, Minnesota. Manufactured by Versa Press on acid-free, 30 percent postconsumer wastepaper.